The Story of Margaret

Darlene Barry

ISBN-13: 978-0-9959362-0-1

DEDICATION

To Mary, the keeper of all my secrets.

And

To my granddaughter Demika, you are my heart.

DEDICATION

To Mary, the keeper of all my secrets.

And

To my granddaughter Demika, you are my heart.

ACKNOWLEDGMENTS

Thank you to Candace and Janice for helping me, believe in me!

Darlene Barry

CHAPTER ONE

Sitting in her rocking chair, looking out the window toward the water, Margaret wondered why she was thinking so much of the old days, of things long gone, and some things that were best forgotten. She had sat in this chair, looking out over the water many times over the past eighty years. Many of those years watching for a sight of Frank's boat. A sign, telling her he was on his way in from a long day of fishing, and on his way home to her and Michael, their son, and their cozy home on the banks of Pleasant Cove, in Newfoundland.

Michael was married and lived with his wife in St. John's. He met his wife Janet at law school, and they married just before they graduated. Janet came from a family in Ontario and was such a beautiful girl. Margaret remembered how proud she and Frank were when Michael passed his bar exam and, even happier when he decided to open his practice in St. John's. He said it was important to him that he live and work in Newfoundland. Michael had a successful law firm, and

Janet worked at the university as a professor, but her passion was writing.

Margaret remembered the first time Michael brought Janet to Newfoundland after they were engaged.

"Have you ever had Newfie Steak, me Darling?" Frank asked.

"No, but Michael said he loves it, so I'm sure I will."

The look on Janet's face when a plate of fried bologna, boiled potatoes, and mustard pickles was placed in front of her was something Margaret would never forget.

She looked at Michael as if to ask, "What is this?"

Michael smiled and said, "Be glad Dad didn't decide your first Newfoundland meal was to be fish heads, cod tongues or fish and brews. Otherwise, you may have run from the Island screaming."

They laughed, enjoying their simple supper and Janet declared she loved Newfie steak, and the rhubarb and apple pie was fantastic.

As she rocked, she thought of her life over the years. There were hard times, but blessings as well. One of those blessings was her granddaughter Lacy.

She loved that child with all her heart, and Lacy loved to listen to Margaret talk about the old days.

Maybe that was why she was thinking about them so much.

Lacy wanted to be a writer like her mother, and she wanted to write a story of someone important to her. Margaret had suggested her grandfather, but Lacy said,

"You can't get first had information from a dead person Gran. I want to hear about your life. Then, if I have questions, you can answer them."

As Margaret rocked, the wind outside brought whitecaps to the water and her mind drifted.

The day was full of sunshine as she ran along the banks of the ocean. The gentle breeze blew her hair behind her, and nothing was more enjoyable than to find a comfortable spot, lay down on the sweet smelling grass with a good book, and enjoy the sound of the water.

Margaret loved reading and getting lost in a world of romance and intrigue. She Found a spot where the grass was high and settled in to read. Lost in the story of Grace Cameron, a reporter whose husband had died in a plane crash, Grace was still having a hard time dealing with his death that happened almost two years ago. Grace decides to get away for a while in hopes of finding peace and takes an extended vacation in Greece. There she meets Marco, the property owner of the house she will be renting for the next six months.

As in all Harlequin stories, Margaret knew where the encounter would lead. However, it was the story of getting there that she loved. She is always acutely aware of the sounds around her and today was no different. In the middle of a sentence, she stopped reading. Hearing the soft wind and the soft swish of grass moving, she froze like a rabbit, hoping that whatever predator lurked would pass and not notice her. Closing her book, she waited. She picked a spot where the grass was the highest, but this, she knew, didn't always work. As a shadow blocked the sunlight, she was on her feet as quick as a wink. But it was not fast enough. Jarred Brown grabbed her and pushed her to the ground.

"Well now, what are you doing here, Margaret? Waiting for me, were you?"

"That will be the day! Now get off of me."

Fear was starting to build inside her, but she was not going to let him know. He pushed her into the soft grass, and she could feel him grow.

"Get off Jarred, or I swear I will yell."

"And if someone were to come, I would just tell them I was sleeping right here in the grass enjoying the day and you came and lay right on top of me."

As she struggled, she could feel the burn mark on her wrist where he pulled her arms above her head, forcing himself on top of her tiny frame. She knew hating was a sin, but she did hate him. She never understood how he knew where to find her because she always tried to find the best hiding places. It seemed nowhere was safe. He soon had his sport, and with an ugly grin on his face released her.

"Now remember Margaret, if you say a word, I'm going to say it was your fault. And, good god girl, your father will beat you silly. Besides, imagine all the trouble you would cause, and for what?"

She heard his laughter as he walked away. As she pulled down her dress, she tried hard to fight back the tears. She could never say Jarred raped her because he never let things go that far. However, the feel of him next to her panties made her sick. She hated all of them. As long as she could remember she was the target of disgusting men who would come and visit her father, laugh, and joke like they did nothing wrong. Jarred was right, she couldn't tell. There would be trouble, and of course, it would be all her fault. Her sisters would blame her if she told them how their husbands always tried to get after her. She knew her best friend would hate her if. No! She was not going to think about that.

"One day, she thought, I will be far away from here and far away from them."

As Lacy lay back down in the grass, warm tears flowed

down her cheeks. She forced herself to listen to the soft sound of the wind and the water. She lost herself in a world where she was safe, happy, and undamaged.

Margaret woke with a start. Where was she? Why was her face wet? She had apparently fallen asleep here in the rocking chair, and slowly, ever so slowly, she remembered. She knew why her face was wet.

It was dark outside, and she could no longer see the water, but she could hear its gentle sound. It soothed her as it always had. She tried so hard to put these things out of her mind. Over the years, she had managed to find ways to do that. Now she found she was thinking back too much. She looked at the clock and saw it was near midnight.

"I have to get to bed," she thought. Her mind began to wander back again. Frank Blanchard was a man who believed in early rising. She smiled when she thought of how Michael hated to wake up on a Saturday morning after being out with his friends the night before.

"Get up, my boy! If you want to stay out until the moon is ready for bed, get used to saying hello to the sun."

It used to drive Michael crazy!

She undressed and pulled on her favorite nightgown and crawled into bed. Frank was gone these past ten years but she couldn't get used to sleeping on his side of the bed. She liked to fall asleep with her arm resting on his pillow. Frank could be difficult, but he brought out the best in her, and Margaret liked to think she brought out the softer side of him. She snuggled tighter to his pillow. It was one of those nights where she missed him more than other nights.

She felt her body relax and knew sleep was on its way. Maybe she would meet Frank along the moonbeams in her dreams. The night moved on, and she dreamed she was walking in a field of flowers. The smell of the ocean drew her out toward the cliff. Standing on the bank overlooking the sea, she put her hand up to her forehead to shield the sun and looked out over the water. There she saw Frank standing on the boat waving to her. He was speaking to her, and the wind carried his words to her as clear as if he were whispering in her ear.

"Soon, my Maggie, I'll miss you no more. I'll walk just beyond the moon, and then I'll stop, and wait for you."

The vision began to fade as she slowly turned and walked back toward the house.

CHAPTER TWO

Lacy paced the floor of her apartment experiencing what she thought was writer's block. She wanted to write a book about her grandmother. After all, her grandmother was one of the most amazing women she knew. Lacy felt there was so much more that her grandmother could tell her, but seemed reluctant to do so. She talked freely and openly about her life with her grandfather. However, when Lacy would question her about her childhood and early teen years, it was limited information she gave. Lacy decided it was time to talk to her dad.

"I just feel like Gran is not completely open with me when I ask her questions. One day I asked her to tell me about things she liked to do as a young girl, and she said she loved to read. Anyway, she talked about her love of reading, how it could take you away to fabulous places you may never get to see in your lifetime.

I asked where her favorite reading place was and she got a very strange look on her face and said,

"Where ever I could be left alone in peace."

"And then she changed the subject."

Michael smiled as he listened to his daughter talk. He knew she didn't realize just how much she and her gran were alike.

"I just found it a bit of an odd comment."

Michael stared at his daughter and knew the puzzle would drive her nuts.

"I understand you want your book to be as honest and as accurate as you can make it. However, you have to accept the answers your grandmother gives you. Your gran is a very private, proud person, and there may be things she just doesn't want to share."

The truth of this struck home. She had such an open and honest relationship with her grandmother that she told her everything. Lacy remembered the day she told her grandmother about Scott Lambert, a music teacher at her high school, who cornered her one day in music class after everyone left. She was practicing on the piano for an upcoming show with her school but was having difficulty with the piece.

"Need some help?"

"Maybe. I can't seem to get this one piece right."

"No problem. Let me assist you." He stood behind her

and placed his hands on the keys.

"Place your hands over mine and feel the flow of the movement. The tune has to flow."

Putting her hands over his as his fingers found each key, she could feel the change from one note to the next.

"That's it! That is the part I couldn't get"

"You'll get it with just a bit more practice."

Before she knew what was happening, he lowered his mouth to the side of her neck. In an instant, she slammed the cover of the piano on his hand and swung around.

"You bastard! How dare you! If you ever try any shit like that again, I'll report you."

"Please Lacy, you're overreacting. I didn't mean any harm. Besides, if you tell, who would believe you?" he said, holding his fast swelling hand.

"I don't care who would believe me. The fact is, I know I would be telling the truth, and you sir would be out of a job. And believe me, if you ever come near me in such away again, I will yell from the top of my lungs." She picked up her bag, left the music auditorium, and went directly to see her grandmother.

When Lacy walked through the door, Margaret knew something was wrong, but she would let her talk in her own time.

"Hey there! How was school today?"

"Okay, much the same as any other, I guess."

"The big show will be coming up soon, won't it?"

"Yes, two weeks."

Lacy loved staying at her grandmothers' when her parents were away. Her school was halfway between St. John's where her parents lived and Pleasant Cove where her grandmother lived. It was the perfect solution. Mr. George, her dad's friend, had to pass right by her school on his way to and from work, so when she stayed at her grandmothers', he gave her a ride back and forth.

Sitting at the piano in the living room, she brushed her fingers over the keys. "Gran, I have to tell you something. I can't tell Mom and Dad because they will go off the deep end and I don't want that."

"Here it comes," thought Margaret.

Lacy told her grandmother everything that had happened. Margaret felt a rage fill her soul. Yet, at the same time, she was filled with pride.

"Good for you Darling. You handled yourself well."

"But Gran, you can't tell Mom and Dad."

"I'll not say anything to your parents this time, but if he or anyone ever tries to do something like this again, you will have to tell."

Her grandmother said this with such force that it surprised her. However, she promised. Later, when Lacy went up to her room to do homework, a plan was already forming in Margaret's head.

The next day, bright and early, Margaret made a trip to the school. She found Mr. Lambert sitting in his office looking over sheet music.

"Good morning Mrs. Blanchard. Are you looking for Lacy? Classes don't start for another hour."

"My goodness, Mr. Lambert, what happened to your hand?"

"Aw, well I was very careless yesterday, and I jammed a ladder on it."

Margaret just looked at him until he turned his eyes away.

"Mr. Lambert, I didn't come here to look for Lacy. In fact, I don't want her to know I was here at all. I've come here to see you. To tell you that if you ever so much as touch a hair on her head, you will need to come up with a better story than getting your hand caught in a ladder because I will be your worst nightmare. Do I make myself clear?"

She turned to walk out of his office.

"I don't know what Lacy has told you."

Margaret swung around with pure fury on her face.

"Don't you dare say she lied. Lacy does not lie, and I've known far too many men like you in my life. Touch her again and I assure you, you will pay the price."

She turned and walked out of his office and out of the school. She wished she would of had Lacy's courage when she was a child.

A few weeks later, Lacy came home and told Margaret that Mr. Slime bag Lambert had transferred to a school in Corner Brook.

"Good riddance to bad rubbish," said Margaret.

CHAPTER THREE

Very slowly, as Margaret began to wake, she was instantly aware of the presences of Frank. She pulled his pillow over to her face, and she could swear she smelled his scent, just like he did when he would walk into the house from being out on the water. It was the most beautiful smell of air and salt. Getting herself ready for her day, she found herself humming *Just Beyond the Moon.* She wondered what made her think of that old Tex Ritter song.

Frank loved the words of this song. *I'll walk just beyond the moon, and then I'll stop and wait for you.* Maybe she was humming it because of the dream she had of Frank last night.

In the kitchen making her breakfast, Margaret remembered that Lacy would be coming over later in the afternoon. She was working on her book and would have a million questions. Having made a promise to her the day she was born to love her forever and never lie to her, it was difficult when Lacy asked questions about her childhood.

When she asked her something she wasn't comfortable with, Margaret just found a way to answer without lying.

She put the kettle to boil, looked out the kitchen window and thought, "I'd better get that garden weeded today before you can't see a rose bush anywhere."

With her breakfast over, she tidied up and got ready for the garden. A quick look at the clock showed 8:30 a.m., lots of time to get her gardening done before making lunch. Moving through the garden, pulling weeds and humming, she felt tightness in her chest. It wasn't a pain exactly. It just felt uncomfortable and was more frustrating than anything.

Michael and Janet worried about her living alone and wanted her to go live with them, but she was happy where she was. She loved the quiet, loved her space, and doing things in her own time. Giving the garden the once over, she was now satisfied that the roses would breathe again. She turned and went into the house.

With her hand to her chest, she went to her rocking chair and sat. Her gaze turned to the window. Slowly the discomfort eased off, but lord almighty, she was tired all of a sudden.

She opened the window a crack and felt the beautiful air flowing from the ocean.

"My, but that feels nice!" she thought as she laid her head back and closed her eyes. Then, off to the past, her mind ventured again.

"It's going to be a beautiful church," thought Margaret, as she watched the deliverymen bring the huge rolls of carpet inside.

"I wonder what color the carpet is going to be?" said Mallory.

"Something dark, I guess. That way you can't see the dirt as much."

Mallory Johnson was her best friend. She was a little bossy at times, but Margaret just let her have her way unless it was something of great importance to her. Mallory was like a sister, and they spent all of their time together. She used to sleep over at Mallory's house more than she did her own.

Margaret's relationship with her father was always tense, and it seemed while she could do nothing right, her sisters could do no wrong. She learned early on to stay out of his way. When she and Mallory became friends, Mallory's father took a liking to her. He treated her just like one of his kids, and she loved him with all her heart.

One night, she and Mallory were going to a dance. They left the house and started walking down the drive.

Suddenly she remembered that she had left her watch on the counter top when she was doing the dishes.

"Oh, darn. I forgot my watch. I'll just run back and get it. It will only take me a minute."

"Hurry up. We don't want to miss the bus."

Mr. Johnson was sitting in his usual place at the table.

"Hi! I just forgot my watch, and I feel lost without it. Okay, I've got it, see you later."

"Wait a second, don't I get a hug goodbye?"

Margaret thought this was an odd remark, but thought she was just being silly. She walked up and put her arms around him and then she felt his hand slip along the side of her breast. She pulled back quickly and in a small voice said, "How could you? I expect it from everyone else but never you."

Shocked and sickened at the same time, she ran out of the house. It would be the last time she would sleep at her friend's house.

The two girls ran to catch the bus, but for Margaret, the evening was ruined.

"Why?, she asked herself, Why?"

Even though they were close to the same age,

Margaret was more physically developed than Mallory. She would have loved to tell her friend that it was more burden than a blessing. But she could never share that with Mallory. She would go to the dance tonight, and act like everything was okay.

The dance finally ended, and they boarded the bus to go home.

"Glen seemed happy you were there tonight," said Mallory.

"You think so?"

"Sure, he didn't want to dance with anyone else once he saw you, silly."

"I think I'll go home tonight," said Margaret.

"Why?"

"Just want to. You can sleep at my house if you want."

"No. Tomorrow is Saturday, and you know my mother. Clean, clean and more cleaning," said Mallory.

"Okay. I'll see you tomorrow," said Margaret.

The girls went in separate directions, and though they remained friends for years, Margaret never did sleep at Mallory's again.

Mallory would never know what happened when she

went back to get her watch.

CHAPTER FOUR

"Gran, are you in here?" Lacy was yelling as she was walking through the house.

Margaret woke and looked at the clock. My God, it was going on 11:30 a.m., she couldn't believe she had fallen asleep.

"In here, Lacy."

Lacy walked into the room, and she noticed that her gran looked tired.

"Did you not sleep well last night, Gran?"

"Well, it was a little later than usual, but I slept okay. I guess being eighty is starting to catch up with me."

Lacy looked at her gran and for one second felt the urge to rush and wrap her arms around her and never let her go. This amazing woman had always been her strength and her confidant. The force of love she felt for her took her breath away.

"I was planning on making lunch for us. Are you hungry?"

"That's okay, Gran. I ate not long ago. Why don't we sit out back in the garden?"

They walked to the back garden that faced toward the water and sat at the old table.

"So, what is it you want to talk about today? By the way, how's the book coming along?"

"Well, I seem to be at a wall right now. My mind keeps racing forward, but when I put my fingers on the keyboard, it goes silent inside my head."

"I think you have what they call writer's block, my dear."

"Hmm, maybe. Let's get started shall we?"

"Sure. Where to today?"

"Well, let's pick up where we left off last. You were telling me about the new church."

"Oh, yes. It was something. Back in my day, the church was the cornerstone of everything. The schoolhouse I went to only had one teacher but she taught three grades at the same time."

By the time my sisters and my nephews got there, she was teaching the third generation of my family."

"Wow! That is dedication."

"The school was right next to the new church, so we were all excited to see the progress each day."

Lacy watched her gran's face change, and she waited until she was ready to speak again.

"The church had two big oak doors and stain glass windows. To me, it was the most unique and beautiful thing in the world. Mallory and I were watching one day as the deliverymen were bringing in the huge rolls of carpet. We were guessing as to what the color would be. Back in those days, the church doors were never locked, so later that afternoon, I went back to the church. I felt the need to go inside. This need was so strong that it seemed as if an invisible rope was pulling me. I walked up to those doors and walked inside."

"The smell of new wood, the soft sea green color of the walls created a heavenly space. Over in the corner against the wall were the rolls of carpet. I walked over and rubbed my hand along the course undercoating. I felt special as I turned back the corner to see the color of the carpet. It was a dark green like when the sea is getting ready to roll. There was a silence in the church, and as I looked toward the newly constructed altar, I felt drawn. I walked up and on the wall was the most beautiful cross bearing the broken body of Jesus."

"It seemed like he was looking right at me. I felt He could hear my heart. I prayed then, truly prayed.

The sun was pouring in through the windows, and it seemed like the sun was coming directly from heaven. I felt warm, safe and happy."

Margaret talked on for about an hour more. Telling stories and watching Lacy absorb them like a sponge. The click of the recorder confirmed the end of the tape. Lacy took it out and turned it over.

"Lacy, I'm not sure how any of these old stories are going to help with your book."

"Well, when we talk, I later go back and listen to the tapes. Anyway, beyond what I will use for my book, I look at each of these tapes as gifts. This way, I will always have your voice and your stories; I'll always have you, Gran."

"Lacy, you are my heart. You don't need tapes and stories to keep me near you, though that is fine as well. I will always be in your heart. After I leave this earthly place, in every ray of the sunshine you see, you will know that it's me smiling on you. I will always be near."

"I love you so much, Gran. I just can't imagine my life without you."

"Well, child, I've always told you nothing on this earth lasts forever, nothing good or nothing bad and that includes people as well."

"Don't cry for my leaving when the time comes.

Cry with joy for I will be with my Frank and my Lord. Just think as if I'm gone on an extended vacation until you can visit me. I want a very long and full life for you, my girl, so make sure you don't visit too soon after I'm gone. Come on now. I'm all done for today. I need some lunch."

Lacy helped her gran up out of the chair and arm in arm they walked toward the house. Lacy noticed her step was slower these days, but she was eighty, after all. They made lunch together and talked about different things. They talked about neighbors and friends of the family. Then her grandmother got around to asking about John Sinclair. Lacy had met John through her friend Mandy, and they had just started a relationship.

Lacy laughed and said, "We're doing just fine. Nothing rushed, just having fun."

"Well, you could do worse than John Sinclair. I knew his grandfather when he first started Sinclair Import/Export, and if John is like his grandfather and father, he comes from good stock."

"He is a good man, Gran. I'm just not ready to settle down yet. There is so much I want to do, and John is just starting at the company, so there's lots of time."

"Yes, a lot of time, but is there still enough time for me to see you happily married? She wondered where that thought came from, for she was not one to be morbid. Gosh, she was being silly these days. They finished lunch and Lacy started to remove the dishes.

"Just leave them, dear, it will give me something to do later."

"Are you sure?"

"Very much. Now get yourself ready and off you go. I don't like you driving into Clancy after dark. It's an exposed portion of the road from here in the cove to Brian's turn before you get to Clancy."

"I know, Gran, and I will be careful. I'll call later."

Margaret watched her go, and she felt very melancholy.

"Give yourself a shake old girl and get over this nonsense," she said to herself.

CHAPTER FIVE

Lacy's grandmother was very much on her mind as she drove home. She seemed more tired than usual and She decided she was going to talk to her dad about her gran. But for now, she had to get home and ready for her date with John.

As she was putting the key into her door she could hear the phone ringing. By the time she had got in, the machine had picked up and she heard John's smooth voice.

"Hi. I hope you didn't forget our date tonight. I'll pick you up at eight."

Hmm, no I miss you, cannot wait to see you. Well, that was John, unemotional and straight to the point. Sometimes, she wondered if he dated her because he liked her or because of whom her parents were.

Michael Blanchard was a very prominent criminal Lawyer in St. John's. Her mother, Janet, was born in Ontario and moved to Newfoundland when she married her dad.

She was teaching Law at Memorial University in St. John's, as well as, a published writer of historical romance.

Lacy smiled when she thought about her grandfather telling the story of her mother's first dinner with the family.

"Probably was the only case of a mainlander turned Newfie on the spot there ever was," he said.

Her grandfather had a wonderful sense of humor and was always so kind to her.

It was now 5:30 p.m. Lacy had time for a nice long bath before John came to pick her up. She decided she would give her mother a call first. Janet picked up on the first ring.

"Hey, Mom."

"Hey, yourself. What have you been up to today?"

"I was out visiting gran, and I'm a little concerned about her."

"Why, is she sick?"

"No, she just seems fatigued."

"Well, Lacy you have to remember your gran is old,

"I know, but she always looks so full of life it is hard to see her this way. Anyway, I was just really calling to check in and say hi. I've got to get ready for my date with John."

"Oh how nice, well, have fun and call me tomorrow."

"Okay. Bye."

Mother and daughter hung up the phone but each were having mixed feelings about gran. Janet loved her Mother-in-law. She had married Michael at 23, and after 30 years of marriage, she was still madly in love with him. And in all that time, not one cross word had ever been exchanged between her and her in-laws. She was devastated when Frank passed away. He always said he gained a daughter when Michael married her. She made a mental note to speak with Michael about his mother.

Back at the house, Margaret was setting the table for supper. Mallory was coming for a visit. Inner Harbour was only an hour from Pleasant Cove but Mallory did not like to drive after dark so she would be spending the night.

It was hard to believe they were still friends after all these years. Mallory had moved away to New York when she married Gerald Richards, a very well to do real estate tycoon. She had met Gerald when he had come to the island for some reason or other, and until she agreed to marry him, he always seemed to find a reason to visit.

Gerald was a man who liked to have a woman in every town where he sold real estate. When Mallory found out, she made him pay handsomely. She walked away and never looked back. Margaret tried to console her when it happened. However, Mallory was having none of that. She never remarried, but over the years, she had some close friends.

As for Margaret, Frank was the only man for her. He was all she ever wanted and knew her life would never be the same from the moment they met all those years ago at the dance. She often thought back to the day as a young girl, sitting on the huge roll of carpet in the newly built church, if God had heard her prayer and Frank was his answer.

She was taking the loaves of homemade bread out of the oven just as Mallory walked through the front door.

"God almighty it smells wonderful in here," said Mallory.

She walked over to Margaret and gave her a hug.

"Aw, it's good to see you, Maggie, it seems like it has been forever."

"Well, I hope you're hungry I've got a pot of scrapper stew, fresh bread, and apple pie for dessert."

"I'm starved."

"Put your things in the bedroom, then come, and sit."

The two old friends sat, ate, and talked. They caught up on old times, talked about old friends, still here and some long gone. Through the evening, Margaret couldn't shake the feeling that Mallory's visit was more than just a casual visit.

"How's Lacy doing?"

"She is excellent, and as usual, working on her book about me no less. Not sure how exciting that will be."

"She has talent all the same. I have read some articles she has written for the newspaper on different happenings. She is good. She makes things clear, concise and to the point."

"Well, her mother is a teacher and writer, after all, so I guess she comes by in honestly."

"Yes, I suppose so."

"Let's have our tea in the back garden."

"Sure, I'll bring the desert and you bring the tea."

As Margaret watched Mallory gathered up the teapot and the teacups, she noticed how badly her hands were shaking.

Margaret and Mallory sat outside and drank their tea enjoying the quiet. They did not feel the need to make conversation if they did not want to. It was like that between them, it always had been.

They enjoyed each other's company and were so comfortable. However, this night Mallory wanted to talk, to reminisce, and to share.

"Do you remember the time when we were kids, and we watched the men bring in the huge rolls of carpet to the church?"

"Yes, said Margaret. It's funny you should mention that. I was sharing that story with Lacy only today."

"I knew you went back there that afternoon."

"You did?"

"Yes."

"Why didn't you come with me?"

"I don't know, I was going to but somehow I felt like it was something you had to do on your own."

"Yes. I guess it was."

"We have shared many things over the years, you and me, Margaret."

"Yes. Indeed we have, and I thank God every day he gave me such a friend as you. I don't know what I would have done without you when Frank passed. It was a hurt so deep that I thought for sure I would never come out of it. It will be ten years this August, and there is never a day that goes by I don't miss him."

"Are you sorry you and Frank never had more kids?"

"No. Not really. Michael was such a wonderful boy, and he turned into such a fabulous husband and father."

"What about you? Are you sorry you choose not to have kids?"

"No. I can't say I am. I have lived a good life, came, and went as I pleased, been blessed with a few good friends, and a few good lovers along the way," she chuckled.

"But no, I can leave this earth happy with my decisions. However, some things that have happened in my life I have a hard time living with."

Margaret knew what Mallory was referring to but unless she carried that conversation further. Margaret would leave it alone.

"Well, what has been happening in Inner Harbour these days? I know it is only an hour away, but I never feel the need to leave Pleasant Cove."

"Not much really, Nancy Walters broke her hip last month and had had to move in with her son and his wife."

"Oh my, from what I remember Nancy and Paula mixed like oil and water."

"That's for sure."

"I heard Harold Skinner, who owns the bar, said he is going to have to charge Jake Walters rent if he doesn't go home."

The time flew by quickly. After cleaning up the dishes, they decided to play some cards for a couple of hours.

"Well, that's it for me old girl," said Mallory. "I'm off to bed."

"Yes. Me as well," said Margaret

They tidied up and said their good nights and each went to their room.

As Mallory got ready for bed, she thought, "I should have told her. If it were her, would I not want to know?"

Margaret could not shake the feeling that something was not right with Mallory, But she could not put her finger on it. Well, if it were anything important Mallory would tell her for sure. She got herself ready for bed, and within minutes, she was asleep.

The morning came filled with sunshine. Margaret had breakfast waiting for Mallory as she came into the kitchen.

"Margaret it always smells so wonderful in your kitchen."

"It's just some bacon, eggs, and toast. I know you always like to set out early and I don't want you leaving on an empty stomach."

"Fat chance of that around here!"

They ate their breakfast, and afterward, Margaret walked Mallory out to her car.

"You call as soon as you get home, you hear."

"Yup. Sure will."

Mallory turned around and looked at Margaret. "You know how much I love you right? How dear you are to me?"

"Yes. Of course, I do silly. And I love you too. Mallory is everything okay?"

"Yes. It was just important that I tell you. I'll call later."

Mallory pulled out of the drive, and Margaret still could not shake the feeling there was something that Mallory was not telling her.

The drive back to Inner Harbour was a beautiful one. Mallory's mind kept wondering, and she knew she should have told Margaret. But what good would it have done, she would have only worried and fretted. All of Mallory's family were long gone, and Margaret was as close as a sister was without being blood-related.

She remembered the night Margaret had met Frank Blanchard. One could not help notice him. His hair was jet black, and his eyes were as blue as the sky on a summer's morning. She was so happy that Margaret and Frank had so many wonderful years. If there was anyone who deserved some happiness in this life, it was Margaret. Mallory knew of the abuse Margaret had suffered over the years. However, it was not because they talked about it. They did not. Mallory knew because she found out by accident.

Margaret's favorite thing to do was read and lounged in the tall soft grass. Mallory was sure that was where she would find her, most likely lost in a book. It was on such a day that she saw Jarred Brown walking away and laughing, and she saw Margaret stand up and pull down her dress. She wanted to rush to her. But Mallory knew that it would be more shame than Margaret could bear. She had heard stories about Jarred Brown, and now, she knew why he was walking away from Margaret laughing. Mallory sat in the tall grass and waited for what had to be close to an hour, and then she stood up and started yelling out Margaret's name as if she had just come looking for her.

After a few minutes, Margaret stood up and yelled.

"Over here."

"Gee, I was wondering where you were, come on let's go get something to eat I'm starving."

They talked about other things, but not about what happened. After that day, Mallory always tried to be with Margaret when she went reading, even if it meant reading a book she found silly. At least this way she could protect her a little, and to Mallory, it seemed they shared an unspoken secret. Now she was keeping a secret from Margaret again. Again, thinking it was in her best interest. Only time would tell.

CHAPTER SIX

Janet was in bed when Michael came home. He was working on a case that was taking up much of his time. These things she understood. Many times, they talked about his cases, debated, and at the end of it, fell into each other's arms, loved, and fell asleep.

"Hey there, you're still up."

"Yes. I want to talk to you about something."

"Yeah. What's that?"

"Your mom."

"What about her?"

"When Lacy was visiting she said she looked fatigued. Maybe we should see if we could get her to move in with us."

"Janet, you know Mom is not leaving her home. She is where she wants to be, and let's face it; she would hate St. John's. To her Pleasant Cove and St. John's are worlds apart."

"I know Michael but I worry about her out there alone."

"She is not alone, we are only a phone call away, and she has tons of neighbors. But I'll call Mom this week and see about going down on Sunday. I know she would like that, and it will give us an excuse to check on her."

"Why Mr. Blanchard you are so smart. It must be the reason I married you!"

As Michael slid into bed beside his wife, all thoughts of his mother and everything else slipped away. He didn't care why she married him, he was just thankful that she had.

The morning sun rose like a brilliant light. Margaret dressed and planned to get some things done around the house. But they could wait until she had her cup of tea. The ringing of the phone startled her and she quickly picked it up before it got to ring for the third time. She was pleasantly surprised to hear Michael's voice on the other end.

"Hey, Mom."

"Hey yourself, what do I owe the pleasure of your call?"

"Oh come on Mom it is not like I never call."

"You're right, you're a good son, and you do check on me often. Is this what you're doing today, checking on me?"

"Yes and no, Janet and I were thinking of coming down on Sunday for a visit if that's okay."

"Oh Michael that would be wonderful. I'll make a nice big dinner. Make sure you call Lacy and get her to come as well."

"I don't think that will be a problem. She spends all her time with you working on her book."

"Yes. She does visit me a bit. I'm such a lucky Gran don't you think?"

A day with her family how precious, she was already thinking of what she would make.

Lacy planned to drive down and see her grandmother today and hoped she would be in a talkative mood. Pulling her long blond hair into a ponytail, she picked up her bag and was just ready to walk out the door when the phone rang.

"Hello."

"Lacy dear I was wondering if you were still planning on coming down to see me today."

"I'm just walking out the door actually. Why?"

"I was just wondering. I have to go over to see Mrs. McCarthy for a while this afternoon she is not feeling well and I've made her a pot of soup. I won't be too long."

"Okay Gran. Bye."

It had been a couple of weeks since her last visit. As a young girl when her parents would go away on business, she would stay with her grandmother and every day was an adventure.

On her drive from Clancy to Pleasant Cove, Lacy thought about what she wanted to ask her grandmother today. Pulling her car into the driveway of her grandmothers' house always gave her the feeling of home and she loved it. She picked up her bag with her tape recorder and went into the house. Grabbing an apple from the fruit bowl on the table Lacy walked out back to wait.

The day was beautiful and the smell of the ocean refreshing. The air was always a little cooler near the water but she loved it. Her mind went back to her date with John the other night. It seemed as if something were bothering him but when she asked, he just brushed it off so, she let it drop.

She wondered if maybe he wanted to stop seeing her and didn't know how to say it. No. John Sinclair was a man who did not have trouble speaking his mind.

She knew she would not be seeing him next week as he was away on family business.

She heard her gran coming in and yelled out, "I'm out here."

Margaret walked to the back and took a chair next to her granddaughter.

"You all right Gran?"

"Yes. I'm just a little out of breath. I was hurrying to get back. Be a good girl will you and bring me out a glass of lemonade. I made a new jug this morning."

Lacy went into the kitchen, got the lemonade and two glasses from the cupboard, and went back out to the garden. As she walked through the door, she saw her gran with her hand held over her chest.

"Gran, are you alright?"

Margaret quickly dropped her hand. "Yes. I'm still a little out of breath from hurrying home from Mrs. McCarthy's. That poor woman is all alone, so I like to help when I can."

That was her gran, always the helpful soul.

"Your parents are coming down for dinner on Sunday. I hope you'll be joining us."

"Yes. Most likely, I've got a few articles I need to

finish up for the newspaper but I should have that done by tomorrow night."

"Do you enjoy freelance writing Lacy?"

"It pays the bills Gran, and there are some positive aspects. Sometimes, I get to go places I might have never gotten to see. But my heart is in writing. It always has been. And that is what I will be and you, my dear Gran, will be the reason."

"Well now, I don't know about that. What do you feel when you write Lacy?"

"It's hard to explain. I guess it's kind of like when you were a young girl, and you would hide away so you could enjoy your book. It was magical to you. It's kind of like that. Writing is all I can think of, sometimes I wake at night, and some silly thing will come into my head. I just have to write it down because I don't know if it will lead to something later. Why do you ask?"

"No reason. I just wanted to understand a bit better I guess."

"I find writing to be a healing tool. I can put it all down on paper and sometimes, that is enough. I suppose that sounds silly."

"Not at all child, it sounds like a sensible thing to do. An idea was forming in Margaret's head.

"So what adventure do you want to go on today?"

"Well, I was wondering if you could tell me about how you met Grandpa?"

"Your grandfather was one the best things that ever happened in my life. I don't know what I ever did that God graced me with the blessing of being married to him for sixty-two years."

"Well, let's see now. There was a dance one night at the local school hall, and Mallory wanted to go so bad. She had such a crush on Blake Carson, a boy in our school. Honestly, I don't think he even knew we were alive. But Mallory didn't care. That night as Blake Carson walked into the dance hall there was another boy with him. Mallory's heart just about stopped when she saw Blake. Mine, well it rather flipped when I saw the boy standing next to him."

"He had a cocky grin on his face, his hair was as black as coal, and his eyes were the bluest I had ever seen. You have your grandfather's eyes you know. They did their rounds as boys will do, and we never saw them for most of the evening. Mallory was on the dance floor, but to her sad heart, it was not with Blake."

From behind me, I heard a voice say, "That's a beautiful song isn't it?"

"I turned around and looked into eyes that were a sea of blue with the most beautiful face I'd ever saw on a boy. Then he asked me if I would like to dance."

"Well, now I'm not sure if I said yes or nodded my head, or if he just took it for granted that I would. But the next thing I know I'm in his arms on the dance floor and I felt like a queen. When the dance ended, he walked me back to my chair. I expected him to leave but he pulled up a chair and sat next to me. He asked my name, and I told him. He said his name was Frank Blanchard he was here in Inner Harbour visiting his cousin Blake Carson. He said that his family lived a few miles away in a little town called Pleasant Cove, and he was going to be staying a few weeks."

"That's quite a bit of information to give a girl you've had one dance with," I said to him.

"Well, seeing I plan on taking up every free minute of your time while I'm here, I thought it best to let you know," he said with a grin.

She chuckled, thinking of how cocky he was.

"Later, Mallory found her way back to me. When she saw who was sitting beside me, she quickly looked around for Blake. I introduced her to Frank and explained that he was here visiting his cousin. Of course, she wanted to know where Blake was, but had her own question answered when she looked around and saw him over in the corner with Patty White draped all over him.

"Frank had seen the hurt on Mallory's face."

"Don't give him another thought, Frank told her. If he is too stupid to see there are only two beautiful girls in this room and one of them is mine, and you are the other, then he deserves girls like Patty White."

"I quickly pointed out that one dance hardly makes me your girl Mr. Blanchard. But in your grandfather's cheeky way he said,

"Well, maybe not one, but have no doubt, Miss. Margaret Wilson that you will be my girl."

"And that was how it started. I danced ever dance with your grandfather, and at the end of the night, he walked me home."

"He said he would be coming down to Inner Harbour in a few weeks to work for the summer, with his uncle, on the fishing boats. It was one of the most amazing summers of my life. Your grandfather had an incredible, caring heart for a man, or so I though. I guess he somehow knew that Mallory would feel left out if I spent all my time with him. He was always gracious about including her. One time I asked him, if maybe we should try to fix Mallory and Blake up. He said his cousin was not the right person for Mallory. She was too good and kind for Blake. He said he would have no part in putting them together. It was probably for the best because it wasn't long after we heard Patty White was pregnant and Blake was the father."

"He left her, and her family sent her away to have the

baby. I remember the day Frank told me about it. He was angry with his cousin and said he didn't understand how he could just walk away from his responsibilities."

The clicking of the recorder brought both women back to the present.

"I always thought you and Gramps had something so special."

"Yes. We did, and I hope and pray you will find such a Love."

"I don't think that kind love exists anymore Gran."

"It wasn't all a bed of roses Lacy. Your grandfather and I had hard times, as well as good. Occasionally, he could be a difficult person. However, we knew we loved each other and worked through it. Most things worth having are usually the hardest to obtain and keep. Life is hard, and it is not always fair but when you are left with no choice, you must deal with what is left. That is what your grandfather and I did. We dealt with things as they came."

"Well, Gran, I've got to be getting back so I can finish some of those articles for the newspaper. I'll see you on Sunday."

"Lacy, do you have an extra notepad? I can't find mine, and it will save me time from having to go up to the shop to get one."

"Of course, Gran, notepads are something I'm never without."

"Thank you Dear."

Margaret watched as Lacy left the house and drive away. She was already thinking of a special gift she would give Lacy.

CHAPTER SEVEN

The day was beautiful and unusually warm. Margaret decided to take a walk to the family graveyard. She took a bottle of water from the fridge and headed out. Her walk was slow but her footsteps sure. She had made this walk many times over the past ten years. She would visit and talk with Frank, and sometimes, it felt like he was right next to her. Halfway up the hill, the tightness in her chest made her stop. This constant discomfort was starting to get on her nerves. She decided to go see Dr. Edging about it next week. The tightness passed after a bit, and she proceeded. Michael, bless his heart, had a bench ordered and placed near his father's grave for her. He was as thoughtful as his father had always been. She sat and took a long drink of water and rested.

"Lacy came today Frank, I wish you could see the beautiful woman she has turned out to be."

"However, I'm sure you do see. Michael and Janet are coming over on Sunday, and Mallory was here for a visit.

I've often thought how lucky I was that two of the people I loved most in the world loved each other too. She was such a great strength to me when you left. I guess I'm over the anger of losing you but I never stop missing you. I never thought that the infection in your lung would turn so violent, so quickly and take you. But I am grateful that you went away from me in your sleep, lying right beside me, with your arm over my waist the way we had slept for sixty-two years. I couldn't have stood to watch you suffer."

Margaret sat quietly; the lump in her throat was so large from the forcing back of the tears that were always so close when she let herself give into missing him.

When she felt she could speak again, she said, "Lacy wanted to talk about how we met. Did you hear us talk? Yes. I know you did, just like sometimes at night I feel you ever so softly kiss my cheek or brush a strand of hair off my face. Yes, my darling, I know when you are near me. I asked Lacy about her writing today. About how it made her feel, and what she got out of it. She said it gave her sense of peace to put things on paper a form of self-healing if you will. In all the years we were married, I never talked much about my childhood. I think you always knew the reason but didn't want to make me relive it all again by the telling of it. I miss you, Frank. You taught me to love and gave me a safe world to live in. And a son that looks so much like you, that there are times my heart skips a beat when I look at him."

Sitting for a while, with her eyes closed, Margaret enjoyed the warmth from the sunlight on her face. She felt a warm breath of air cross her lips and the scent of Frank so strong, she opened her eyes. Smiling she said, "You're a cheeky bugger! Always ready to take advantage. Oh, but I love you for it."

She blew him a kiss goodbye before walking back to the house. Margaret found comfort knowing that one day she would lay in final rest with her Frank, her husband, her love.

A cup of tea was in order, and then she would set about making the fixings for a bit of supper. She was just pouring the water in the teapot when she heard a car. Wondering if Lacy had forgotten something and came back, she looked out of the window.

There was a car pulling into her driveway. This was definitely not someone from Pleasant Cove, not driving a Cadillac. A tall man with salt and pepper hair got out of the car carrying a briefcase and walked up to the door. Margaret was there to open it before his hand could knock.

"Mrs. Blanchard?"

"Yes. Can I help you?"

"Mrs. Blanchard, my name is Donovan Grant. I'm a

lawyer from New York. May I come in?"

"Yes. Of course, but I can't see what a lawyer from New York would want to see me about. Are you a friend of my son Michael?"

"I do know of your son Mrs. Blanchard, but we're not friends."

"Come into the kitchen Mr. Grant. I was just making a cup of tea, and you may as well join me."

"Thank you."

As Margaret poured the tea, Donovan Grant brought some papers out of his briefcase.

"So, Mr. Grant, tell me why you have come all this way to see me."

"Do you live alone Mrs. Blanchard?"

"Yes. Why?"

"Well, Mrs. Blanchard I've come to give you some news and, well, it's not very good. I've been Mallory Johnsons' lawyer for about twenty years, and it is with great sadness that I'm here to tell you she has passed away."

The shock on Margaret's face was so evident that Donovan got out of his chair and stood beside her.

"That can't be, she was just here for a visit."

As she looked into his face, Donovan's heart hurt for the pain he was causing this woman. He had tried to talk Mallory out of doing things this way but she was stubborn and would have none of it.

"I'm so sorry Mrs. Blanchard."

"But how? What happened?"

"Mallory was not feeling well for some time. About six months ago, the doctors told her they had found cancer in her breast and had spread to her lungs. Treatment would have given her maybe an additional six months. She decided to decline all treatment."

As Donovan took his seat, he opened up the file folder.

"Mrs. Blanchard."

"Please, call me Margaret."

"Margaret. I'm here to give you this."

He handed her a sealed letter, and her hand was shaking as she took it.

"Mallory has left her estate to you, and by her estate I mean, her house in Inner Harbour and approximately $200.000 comprised of cash, stocks, and bonds."

"I just don't understand why she didn't say anything to me. Damn her! She didn't give me a chance to say goodbye."

Donovan heard the tremble in her voice and felt sorry for her.

"I have known Mallory for over twenty years. She spoke of you often, and I know she loved you dearly. She had no family left and did not want to be buried with her parents. She loved you like a sister, and I think she felt goodbyes were unnecessary. I have a box of her things in my car to bring to you, but there is one particular request that Mallory had. She did not want you to feel obligated, so alternative arrangements have been made but she wanted to be buried in your family graveyard."

As tears filled her eyes, she placed a hand on her chest and said, "Of course. There is no need for alternative arrangements Mr. Grant. Mallory knew what I would say."

"Well, I'll get everything out of the car. Are you going to be all right? I know this was quite a shock. Is there someone I could call for you?"

"Thank you. Mr. Grant but I'll be fine." Margaret felt numb. Her hand still rested on the envelope with her name wrote across the front in Mallory's elegant style. My God, she loved that woman with all her heart. She was her dearest friend, and now she was gone. Donovan came back into the house and placed a box on the counter and another smaller box on the table.

On the top of the small box was Mallory's name. As

Margaret placed her hands on each side of the box, she lifted it, brought her lips down, and gently kissed the lid.

"My forever friend," she whispered.

Donovan heard her, and he felt his heart constrict for the loss this woman had just received. It was starting to get dark, and he needed to get going but he was reluctant to leave her. She was old and alone and had just received such heartbreaking news.

Margaret sensed his dilemma and wanted to ease his burden.

"Mr. Grant I thank you for bringing me the news, and I guess for bringing me Mallory, she said with a little smile, but I think I would like to be alone now."

"Yes, of course, Margaret. I'm so sorry for your loss."

"As am I, Mr. Grant. Thank you."

"I'll call your son tomorrow to discuss the transfer of assets."

"Thank you, Mr. Grant. Have a safe trip back to New York."

The tea had grown cold in the cup, and Margaret pushed it aside. She looked at the box on the table and tears slowly fell from her eyes. No more, phone calls, no more visits, no more Mallory.

"You know I loved you and there was nothing you could not have told me, so, why did you not?" she asked.

There was only silence in the room as she placed the urn to the side and rested her hand on the envelope. Margaret could almost picture Mallory with her head bent, writing this last message to her.

Margaret walked over to the mail holder and took out the letter opener, unable to bring herself to tear the envelope that Mallory had so lovingly sealed. Picking up the envelope, she went and sat in her rocking chair. As she slid the letter opener between the flaps, the smell of Mallory's perfume rose to greet her.

"Hello, old girl," she whispered.

Laying the letter opener to the side, she pulled the sheets of rose-colored paper from the matching envelope.

CHAPTER EIGHT

My Darling Dearest Friend:

I know this has been a shock to you, and for that I'm sorry. If I know you, and I do, you are asking why did I not tell you. What good would it have done? I have lived a good, long life, I was blessed in so many ways, but mostly because of you and the special friendship, we shared and loved each other like sisters. The last time I came to visit you, I knew it would be our last. There were things I wanted to say, things I wanted to tell you but I thought it best to wait.

Margaret, I want you to know that I knew about the abuse. I never mentioned it because I always thought if you wanted me to know, you would have told me. I also want you to know that I saw what happened that day in the field with Jarred Brown. Later that evening after we left each other, I was walking home and saw him hitting baseballs in the field. I went over and told him I needed to speak with him. He came over to the fence, and I said, I know what you did to Margaret. I wish you could have seen his face. He went white.

At first, he tried to say I didn't know what I was talking about. I told him I had seen what he did to you and if he ever came near you again, I was going to tell everyone. He just stared and, turned, and walked away. I couldn't help what happened to you that day but I did my best to try to protect you after. I pray it worked.

I have never understood the love you have for God Margaret but it was never something that came between us. You always showed me kindness and never judged or hurt me. Your God made you my angel. You have always said that when we die, we go to heaven. Well, I am not sure where I am going but wherever it is I only hope, you will be there one day.

As you know, I have left everything to you. I took care of many things at the house, so there should not be too much to do. You can sell it if you want, or give it to Lacy. Whatever you decide is fine.

In the box that Donovan gave you, are some treasures that I kept over the years. One of them is a small square green piece of carpet from the carpet laid in your little church. I knew you felt special seeing the color of the carpet before anyone else, so I wanted to keep it for you.

My dear, dear friend, know that I loved you in life and, in death no less. I am looking forward to seeing your heaven and, when I see Frank, I will give him a hug and kiss for you.

He and I will walk just beyond the moon then we'll stop, and wait for you....

Until me meet again,

Love, your forever friend,

Mallory.

As she folded the letter and placed it back inside the envelope, her tears dropped on the rose colored pattern. Margaret knew she had lost someone so special but decided to not think of it as a lost. Instead, she would think of it as if Mallory had gone on an extended vacation, just like she told Lacy to think of her when she was gone. Margaret envied Mallory this trip, for she would see Frank before her but at the same time, grateful because she knew Frank would be waiting to receive her dear friend.

"How long before I'm with them?" she thought.

Margaret sat for a few moments more and then walked over to the box Donovan Grant had brought in for her. Mallory had marked her name on it, and as she slid her fingers over the writing, she wondered what other treasures Mallory had left her.

Carrying the box, she went to sit in her rocking chair. Margaret's heart was breaking as she sat looking out the window.

"Frank. My darling, please take care of her for me

until I'm with you both."

From across the water, she could see a small dim light. It was as if Frank were winking at her. Pulling back the large piece of tape, she slowly opened the box, folded back the flaps, and gazed at all the treasures inside. There was the small piece of carpet in a plastic bag. She held it in her hands and thought back to that day and the prayer she prayed.

"Lord, if you can hear me, it's Margaret. I know I don't have the right to ask but please, one day bring me someone of my own to love, and someone who loves me. I'm so tired of running. It doesn't matter where I run, they seem to find me, and Lord thank you for my friend Mallory."

Margret remembered how she felt that day. She had always felt like she did not deserve God's love, so for her, it was a brave request.

Tied with a pink ribbon were all the cards she had sent Mallory. She pulled two cards from the stack. One she had sent her for her 50th birthday and, the other a Christmas card. On the inside of each card, she had written the date she received it and a small message.

"I received this beautiful card from Margaret today. It's just like her to never forget an occasion. She is as dear to me as a sister. I love her for so many reasons, one of them is that she shows me her God's Love, even when I don't know if he is there or real."

In the other, she had written, "I love my friend Margaret because, in spite of all the hurts she has endured, she is still such a warm, loving person."

Margaret was surprised and pleased that Mallory thought of her this way. She put the bundle of cards aside and decided she would read one every night before she would go to sleep. It would be a special treat from Mallory to her. What a wonderful gift to receive. Also, inside the box, there were seashells, and on the inside of each one, Mallory had marked a date of when she or Margaret had found them. There was a picture of them at the county fair. Margaret laughed when she remembered that a horse had come very close to christening Mallory. My goodness, she was mad that afternoon. There were also the death notices of her parents. Mallory did not like to talk about her parents much.

The accident had happened when she lived in New York. Malloy had found out about her husband's cheating, and was very upset. She called her mother and told her the news, and that she planned on leaving him. Her parents decided they would go to New York and bring their daughter home. It was late in January, and the road going into St. John's to the airport was like a sheet of glass. In the blinding snow, her father did not see the plow truck coming around the bend. There deaths were instant. Mallory blamed herself for calling them in the first place.

She came home to bury her family and ended her marriage all in one visit.

There were many other trinkets in the box, things that made her smile, and some that brought more tears. She put everything back in the box and laid it beside her chair. She knew she should call Michael but it was late. Nothing was going to change between now and the morning. Nothing was going to bring her friend back. Long into the night, Margaret sat in her chair looking out the window but seeing only things from the past. She pictured her and Mallory as young girls, her and Frank at their first dance and, she even thought about her parents.

Her mother was one of the kindest people she knew and, her father was one of the hardest. She was sure he loved his kids though he wasn't an affectionate man,. They were all gone now, her parents, her siblings, her best friend and her husband. She was the last. She was eighty years old and knew she would not go on forever, but to see Lacy settled would be grand.

Margaret looked over at the box containing Mallory's ashes. She walked to the table and picked up the beautiful box placing it on the mantel in the living room above the fireplace.

"Not too many places I can put you right now Mallory dear, so here you'll stay until I'm ready to let you go."

She kissed her fingers and lovingly laid them against

the box. Margaret turned off the light, walked out of the living room, stopped, went back, and turned on a light on a side table.

"I don't want you in the dark," she said

She got herself ready for bed, and there was a loneliness around her heart that she had not felt since Frank died. With her arm lying over Frank's pillow, she could see the moon shining brightly in the night sky and wondered if they could see her.

This night she dreamed of Frank and Mallory. They were in a field waving at her. She was running as fast as she could but it seemed like she wasn't moving. She heard Frank say to her,

"I'll take care of her for you, my Maggie."

"And I'll take care of him for you dear friend, we love you, Margaret."

Then they faded into a warm glow of light. Slowly Margaret opened her eyes to see the sun pouring through her window. The night had passed, and morning had come. It seemed like only moments ago that she had been with her best friend, and her one and only love.

CHAPTER NINE

Margaret dressed and went into the kitchen to put the kettle to boil. The teacups filled with tea were still sitting on the table from the night before. She dumped them, and placed the cups in the sink. Enjoying a nice cup of tea at her kitchen table, she had a perfect view of the fireplace in the living room.

"Good Morning Mallory," she said. "I know you and Frank are together now, waiting for me. But I've much to do yet old girl, so you'll both just have to hold on a bit longer."

She didn't feel like eating this morning. After drinking her tea, she washed up the few cups and was putting the last one in the cupboard when the phone rang.

"Hello.

"Mom, why didn't you call me last night about Aunt Mallory?"

"It was late Michael and, I needed some time to

digest the information. I take it you have heard from Mr. Grant."

"Yes. This morning. Mom are you sure you're alright?"

"Yes Michael, I'm sure. You can imagine it was a bit of shock but I'm okay."

"Well, if it is okay with you, when we come down on Sunday, I've got some papers for you to sign, there are things you need to know."

"Yes, of course, I'll see you on Sunday."

They said their goodbyes, and she hung up the phone.

Margaret spent the morning in her rocking chair watching the water. Her mind was drifting in all kinds of directions. She got up to get her notebook. Lacy told her writing brought her peace. Well, Margaret was hoping this was true. She sat at her table with pen and notebook and began to write.

Dear ... her words began to fly across the paper. By the time she had stopped writing almost two hours had passed. It was now 4:30 p.m. and, she had just enough time to go over and check on Mrs. McCarthy. Margaret planned to bring her over the casserole she had taken out of the fridge this morning. Margaret felt so sorry for Mrs. McCarthy, she didn't have family near like Margaret. Her son moved to Toronto many years ago but didn't visit much. Her husband died two years ago, and now she was on her own.

On the short walk to Mrs. McCarthy's house, Margaret wondered what Michael, Janet, and Lacy were going to think of the decision she had made.

She gave a courtesy knock and walked inside.

"Margaret, I'm so sorry for your loss."

Margaret never asked how she knew, like everything else in the cove, news spread like wildfire.

"Thank you. It was a bit of a shock."

"Yes. But you and I know what it is to lose someone you love unexpectedly, don't we? When Jim died two years ago, I thought I would die with him. I mean one minute he is out back chopping wood, and I'm inside making his lunch and the next thing I know his heart gave out, and he's dead."

Margaret wanted to change the subject, her loss of Mallory was still too fresh.

"I've brought you a casserole for your supper Mrs. McCarthy."

"That is good of you Margaret. Dr. Edging says I'm doing much better and I'm able to get around a bit, but it hurts like hell fire when I do, so I am grateful that you thought of me."

"It's no trouble at all, but I've got to get going. I'll see you later."

With her goodbyes said she left and began her walk home, saying hello to those she met in passing but her mind was wondering on how she was going to tell Michael, Janet, and Lacy about her decision.

Back at her house, she took out the roast she would be cooking for dinner tomorrow, peeled all her vegetables, and placed them in bowls of cold water. Lifting her big glass bowl out of the cupboard, she began to make pastry dough for a pie. She could have easily phoned the shop and have Walter send one down, but a visit with her family was far too special for anything store bought. Bringing the bowl of apples over to the table, she began peeling and slicing.

"You always said you loved my apple pie, and that I made the best scrapper stew and dough boys you ever had. The one thing no one could ever accuse you of Mallory Johnson is false flattery. We shared many suppers together you and me old friend."

She realized that she was talking to Mallory as if she were just in the other room. It gave her a good feeling and, she knew the decision she had made was the right one. Whether the family agreed or not, she realized she was going to do this. With the apples all cut, she placed the pie in the oven, cleaned up the kitchen, and decided to read for a while.

Picking a book from the many that she had, she sat in her old rocker by the window. Margaret never lost her love of reading or the wonderful feeling of going to some magical place. She needed that for a while, to give her aching heart a rest from the pain of losing her dear friend.

Margaret was lost in a world of romance, this one about Lady Elaine who had been captured by Lord Creighton. She always knew how the story turned out but she loved the adventure of getting there. Before she knew it, the timer went off telling her the pie was ready to come out of the oven. She placed it on the sideboard to cool and enjoyed the aroma of apple and cinnamon filling the room. It was only early in the evening, but she was tired and decided to make an early night of it. She turned off the lights, except the one in the family room for Mallory.

Sitting with pillows behind her back, Margaret pulled over the stack of letters and cards tied with ribbon. She had read some of them already, and they were lovingly placed back in the box, but she promised she would read one each night before she fell asleep in honor of her dear friend.

Tonight she pulled out a card that she had sent Mallory when she lived in New York. It was for her 35th birthday. The front of the card read, I wish we were together on your birthday. With the card, lying on her lap, she whispered aloud.

"Mallory, I wish you were here yourself to tell me what you think of my idea, of what I want to do. I don't want to be selfish."

She opened the card and read what she had written inside, all those years ago, to Mallory, and then she slowly unfolded the note that Mallory had written and placed on the card.

"I received this card from Margaret today. It's Just like her to never forget a special day. Pleasant Cove is a long way from New York but nothing can keep our spirits from being with one another. Not miles, not time, not even death can take away the bond we share, and the knowledge that forever, and always we will do right by one another."

Margaret felt peace enter her heart as soft as a whisper.

"She knew what I was planning, Margaret thought. Thank you, Mallory. You knew I needed to know that what I was doing was right. You have always been there to help me, and this time is no different."

She folded the note back inside the card, placed it under her pillow, lay down to sleep, and was quickly gone into dreams.

She had wonderful dreams of her and Mallory as young girls, running along the water's edge, and in the hospital with Michael, and Mallory telling her what a beautiful son she had. So, continued her night, filled with one memory dream after another, of wonderful times in her life with her friend, whom she loved so much.

The dream ended with her, Mallory and Frank standing on the banks overlooking the water, in a circle, holding hands together. They were young again, and they were together.

Awaking slowly to the sun coming in through the window, she felt happy, rested and at peace. Margaret thought about the special gift of confirmation that Mallory had given her. Even unknowingly, Mallory helped with the decision that to her mind was perfect.

Back in the days of Jarred Brown and the others, her life was hell. It was a life of always running, hiding, and always trying to stay safe. The nightmare had ended when she met Frank and married him in the small church in Inner Harbour. She thanked God each and every day of her life for answering the prayer of the young girl, sitting on a roll of carpet in a church, thinking about how unworthy she was for asking anything of Him. But grateful He loved her in spite of that and answered her prayer.

She didn't like to dwell on those bad times and lying here any longer would do just that. She threw back the covers, got her shower, and started her day. It was 8:15 a.m. when she walked into the kitchen and put the kettle to boil. As she entered the kitchen, the smell of the pie still hung in the air. Michael and Janet would be down early, and they would have an early supper so she would just have some fruit with her tea. The sun was shining but out over the water, the clouds seemed like they wanted to move inland. There was a soft breeze so they would most likely not last. She wanted this day to be perfect.

With time, before the roast had to go in the oven, Margaret went to the cabinet and pulled out her notepad, now known as her journal. And decided to write for a while. As she turned to go back into the kitchen, her eyes fell on the urn.

"I know you, of all people, would have understood and I'm sorry I didn't tell you myself. But the shame kept me from doing so. I didn't want you to think less of me, or our friendship to change. I should have known you would never let that happen. By putting in all down in this journal, perhaps I can make some things right."

Margaret lovingly touched the urn and went back into the kitchen, sat down and continued to write where she left off. After some time had passed, she looked up at the clock, it was going on 10:30 a.m. Margaret ended the sentence she was writing and put the journal away, came back into the kitchen, and began to get the roast ready for the oven. Turning on the radio for company, she began to prepare the meal.

The morning flew by and before long the sound of a car, pulling into the driveway could be heard. Michael and Janet had arrived from St. John's. Margaret wished they would have decided to live in the cove but she understood their work was in St. John's and the hour commute in the winter would have been a nightmare. Having made her peace with their decision, Margaret would enjoy what time they could spare for visits. She watched from the kitchen window as Michael got out of the car, walked around to open Janet's door and extend his hand to help her out.

"We raised quite the gentleman you and me, Frank. My God, he is so much like you."

She heard them come in and Janet flew across the floor to embrace Margaret and give her kisses on both cheeks.

"It smells wonderful in here, and gosh I'm so glad to see you. I know we talk on the phone often, but nothing compares to walking into your kitchen."

"Hi, Mom, Michael said, as he leaned over to kiss her cheek. How are you?"

"I'm okay Michael, don't worry about me."

"Margaret, we are so sorry about Mallory."

"Thank you, Janet. Mallory lived life on her own terms, so why would her death be any different? I was shocked at first when Mr. Grant came to tell me the news, and angry that she didn't tell, me or give me the chance to say goodbye. But everything happens for a reason, even when at the time we don't know what it is."

"Mom, I've brought the papers I need you to sign, and there are some decisions you have to make."

"Let's leave all that until after supper Michael."

From the look on her face and the tone of her voice, Michael knew there was no point in pursuing it now. He would do as she asked and leave it for now.

They sat at the kitchen table and chatted about everyday things. It was good to have them here. Lacy walked into the kitchen just then with a huge smile on her face and In her arms was a beautiful bouquet of fresh flowers.

"For you Gran, I'm so sorry about Aunt Mallory."

"Oh, Lacy they are beautiful! Thank you."

"Show off, her dad said. He walked over to give his daughter a kiss and a hug. How's my girl?"

"I'm Good Dad."

"Hey, Mom," she bent down and kissed her Mom's cheek.

"Well, I'd best get this supper on the table, said Margaret.

It was 3:00 p.m. and she didn't want them driving back to St. John's in the dark. The meal on the table, and grace said, they enjoyed the excellent meal so lovingly prepared. Michael worried that his mother did to much, but he also knew she was a woman who did nothing she did not want to.

If she didn't want to cook, she would have told them. Michael was sure glad she wanted to! The best restaurants on or off the Island, in his opinion, couldn't compare to his mom's cooking. He smiled to himself, it was the same thing he always told Janet but she knew he told his mother the same thing. The truth was they were both amazing cooks.

"How's the book coming Lacy?" asked her mother.

"Slow right now. Gran's great but I'm having trouble placing my sections."

"It will come to you dear," said Margaret.

"It's your fault Gran, you give me so many wonderful stories about your life that I want to make sure I do you justice."

"My life was not all that exciting Lacy but it has been blessed."

They talked about Janet's teaching job and some

freelance legal work; she was doing for a local women's group and the afternoon moved on.

"Let's have dessert in the back garden," said Margaret.

"I'll get the teacups and teapot," said Lacy."

"I'll get the plates and forks," said Janet.

"And I'll bring the pie," said Michael.

"Well, Dad, just make sure it makes it from the kitchen to the garden, untouched!" They all laughed and moved to the back garden.

In the garden sitting at the table with a beautiful view of the ocean, they enjoyed the last part of their supper. Knowing it could not be put off any longer Michael brought the subject up again.

"Mom we have to talk about Aunt Mallory now."

"Yes. I know Michael, and I'm ready now. Afterward, I have something I need to tell all of you."

They all looked at each other and Michael began.

"Well, Mom, Donovan Grant had everything in order on Mallory's end but as your lawyer, there are things I need to register and file. Starting with these bank documents."

He pulled out what looked like banking information.

"Aunt Mallory left you a considerable amount of money, stocks, and bonds. You will need to sign this to have everything transferred to your bank."

Margaret signed without giving it much thought.

"As well, you have to decide about the house in Inner Harbour. Do you want to keep it, or sell it?"

"I guess I'll sell it, I've no desire to live back in Inner Harbour."

"Okay I'll take care of getting it sold but according to Mr. Grant the house is still furnished, even though Aunt Mallory had given away a lot of things."

"Lacy, Janet, would either of you like to have a look before we dispose of the furniture? I'm sure you both will find something you like. Mallory had beautiful taste and a unique quality of bringing old and new pieces together to make every room look like a magazine. I think she found this talent when she lived in New York."

"Thanks, Gran, I would love to."

"Maybe we'll make a Mother/daughter weekend of it Lacy. We can drive up on a Friday night, after work, and back on Sunday and then we can arrange to have what we want to be shipped to us."

"Great idea Mom!"

"Mom, there is one final thing we need to talk about.

I'm sure Mr. Grant told you alternative arrangements have been made for Aunt Mallory if you are not okay with her being buried in our family graveyard."

"How do you feel about that Michael?"

"Well, honestly Mom, it, only seems right. She did request it and she must have given it much thought."

"Yes, she would have for sure," said Margaret. "She has always been such a part of our family, and I'm glad you feel that way because I've made some decisions. Having Mallory with me seems right. So much so, that I've decided not to bury her."

They all looked at her but said nothing. Margaret laughed and said, "Well, not just yet anyway. For some strange reason, I like knowing she is so close to me. It makes the losing of her not so harsh I guess. So, I've decided that Mallory will only be buried when I'm buried. We grew up together, and I want us to be put in the ground, next to Frank, together."

She looked at each of their faces and waited for them to digest this information. Finally, Lacy was the first to speak.

"Gran, I think that is so perfect, and I think Aunt Mallory would like that idea very much."

"Thank you, Lacy. Well, that's settled then."

Janet began clearing up the dishes, and the others

jumped in to help.

"Margaret you just sit, and we'll clean up."

"That would be lovely Janet, thank you."

"Michael, you sit and chat with your mom awhile."

As Janet and Lacy cleared the table and brought the dishes into the house, Michael sat and talked to his mother.

"Michael there is one other thing. You are my only son so, of course, when I'm gone whatever I have will go to you. I want you to arrange my investments, and the stocks, and bonds that Mallory left me as you see fit for you and Janet. I would also like you to set up a trust fund for Lacy with the money Mallory left me and the sale of the house in Inner Harbour."

"Your father, as you know, was a smart man with money. He made sure I would be okay if anything happened to him. For a man who made is livelihood from the water, he did well by us."

"Yes, Mom, I know he did."

"As well as the trust for Lacy, I would like to leave her this house, if you don't mind."

"Mom whatever you decided is okay with me. As long as you're happy, I'm happy."

"I think this house has always been a special place for Lacy."

"She loves it here that's for sure," said Michael.

"The dishes are all done, and I'm sad to say we have to be on our way," said Janet.

"Yes, I don't want you traveling over the roads in the dark."

With kisses and hugs all around, and goodbyes said, the family left to go back to the city.

With a feeling of contentment, she waved until she could no longer see them, turned, and walked back inside. She went into the family room, took the urn off the mantel, and walked to her rocking chair.

"Well, old girl, they took that rather well don't you think? It feels like the right thing to do, you, and me joining Frank at the same time, all three of us together again."

Lowering her head, she gently kissed the name inscribed across the box and placed it on a shelf where she would see it when she was in her rocking chair.

"I like you close to me old girl, and we will have some chats like in the old days."

Rocking back and forth in her rocking chair, she watched the water. It brought comfort as always.

CHAPTER TEN

After arriving home, Lacy wanted to work on her book and to make notes about tonight. Her grandmother was going to miss Aunt Mallory very much. They had always been so close, they were just like sisters. Lacy had friends, but even as dear as Mandy was to her, she didn't know if their friendship would span decades like grans and Aunt Mallory. She hoped it would somehow, it gave her a nice feeling to know there is someone you care about that is such a part of your life's history. Sitting on the sofa with her laptop on her knees, Lacy started to review her notes and do some organizing. Each one came with a memory of her grandmother.

She worked for several hours and was just about ready to take a break when the phone rang. She thought it must be John, so she jumped up to answer the phone.

"Hello."

"Hi Lacy. It's Allan over at Inner Harbour Circle Newspaper."

"Hi Allan. How are you?"

"Fine thanks, but I'm in a bind, and I wonder if you could help me out?"

"Sure Allan what do you need?"

"Well, Kara Sage, one of my local reporters, broke her leg, and she is going to be off for several weeks. We got a hot little story, and I need a good writer. Are you interested?"

"Sure Allan, I could use the work. What's the story?"

"Well, there is an old guy here in Inner Harbour, named Jarred Brown. He's in his nineties and a lifetime resident of Inner Harbour. Linda Godfrey has filed a complaint against him of sexual abuse against her daughter Samantha."

"How old is Samantha?"

"She is only fifteen, and from the bit, I know so far, it has been going on for a few years. The poor kid almost had a breakdown, and finally, she told her Mother. I need a reporter who can cover the story and cover it well. You came to mind right away."

"Thanks, Allan, I'll get on it right away. When were the charges filed?"

"Yesterday."

"I'll come up to Inner Harbour tomorrow and see what I can find out. In the meantime, I'll talk to my grandmother. She grew up in Inner Harbour, I'll see if she knows this Jarred Brown."

"Great, I'll see you tomorrow."

Just the memory of the time Mr. Lambert had touched her still made her sick to her stomach. Lacy couldn't even imagine what that poor girl had endured. She decided she would stop by her grandmothers' tomorrow on her way to Inner Harbour and see if she knew this creep. She decided to make an early night so she could start out early in the morning. She turned off the lights and crawled into her bed.

Her night was restless, and finally, as dawn was breaking she fell into a deep sleep. In her dream, she was walking through her Aunt Mallory's house in Inner Harbour. All the furniture was covered, and the room felt deserted... almost. Somehow, she knew she was not alone. As she walked through the house and up the stairs, she noticed that all the doors were closed except the one at the end of the hallway. This door was slightly ajar. She walked down the hall, opened the door, and gasped. There standing by the window was Aunt Mallory but her form was translucent.

Lacy stopped dead in her tracks and heard Mallory's words though her mouth did not move.

"Be careful what you ask of her Lacy."

Lacy brought her hands up to her eyes, when she took

them down the vision was gone, and she felt like she was flying back in time and woke with a start, with the words fresh in her mind. She lay there for a minute trying to think what the dream meant. Then she decided it meant nothing more than a restless night.

She got showered, made a slice of toast, and got ready to leave. Just as she was about ready to walk out the door, she decided to would call her grandmother and let her know she was coming and why. The phone rang until the machine picked up.

"Hi, Gran it's me. I'm going to be coming over to visit you on my way to Inner Harbour today. I'm doing a story for the paper there on a sexual abuse of a young girl. I was wondering if you remember a man by the name of Jarred Brown. Anyway, you can tell me when I get there. I Love you, bye." She hung up the phone and rushed out the door.

While Margaret worked in her garden, she felt more tired than usual. Her night was full of dreams, and she had not slept well. Margaret just couldn't shake the feeling that something unpleasant was coming.

Giving her garden the once over, she got up slowly and decided a cup of tea was in order. Upon entering the kitchen, Margaret noticed the phone light blinking indicating someone had left a message. Whoever it was, would have to wait until she had made her tea.

Margaret placed her hot cup of tea on the table and

then decided to listen to the message. Oh, excellent! Lacy was coming to visit again. As she listened to the rest of the message, her chest began to tighten. Oh my, God! Lacy couldn't be coming here to talk to her about him. Margaret sat at the table with her hand over her racing heart; somehow, she knew something was coming. By the time on the clock, Lacy would be here in less than an hour. What was she going to say to her? With tea in hand, she moved to her rocking chair and sat looking out at the water. Jarred Brown. He had to be in his nineties for sure. So, his evilness had carried through to his old age. She left Inner Harbour and put that behind her. Mallory never mentioned his name either. But then again, she wouldn't. Now all these years later, he was causing her trouble again, but trouble of a different kind.

She had to force herself to think clearly, to decide what she was going to say. It seemed like hours had passed as she sat looking out the window.

"Oh, Lacy, you don't know what you are asking of me. I don't want to remember."

The sound of a car brought her out of her thoughts, and she knew time had run out. She rose and put the cup in the sink as Lacy walked through the door.

"Hi, Gran. I called, but you must have been outside or somewhere."

"Yes, I was out in the garden."

"They say bad weeds grow fast, and if that's true, the ones in my garden are positively evil because it seems they multiply faster than I can pull them."

"Did you listen to my message?"

"Yes. I did," Margaret said slowly. But I'm not sure I can be of much help to you Lacy. I never went back to Inner Harbour much after I married your grandfather."

"But do you remember a Jarred Brown. I know he is older than you, but Inner Harbour is so small."

"No. I can't say that I do remember anyone by that name."

This was the first lie she ever told her darling Lacy and the pain of it was breaking her heart.

"Too bad Aunt Mallory is not still alive I'm sure she would know him, or of him, at least."

"Yes, she may have."

"I'm sorry I can't be more help dear."

"That's okay Gran I knew it was a long shot, but I thought I would try."

"I'm sorry I can't stay longer. I've got to get back on the road to Inner Harbour.

I want to get there before dark and get checked into the famous Inner Harbour Motel," she said with a chuckle.

"How long are you planning on staying, Lacy?"

"I don't know, a couple of days, or until I get all I can on this story."

"Well, if you're not uncomfortable, why don't you stay at Aunt Mallory's house? It will give you an opportunity to look at the things you and your Mom are going to pick up."

"No, I'm not uncomfortable at all, that's an excellent idea, Gran."

"Hang on, and I'll get you the key."

Margaret went into her bedroom to get the key from her jewelry box on her dresser. She noticed her hand was trembling as she picked up the key, and looked at herself in the mirror.

"Take care of her Mallory, you know what she means to me. Please don't let her find out the truth."

Walking back to the kitchen, she gave Mallory the key.

"Here you go, dear. The power and water are still turned on, so you should be okay."

"Thanks, Gran. I'll call you later."

After goodbye kisses and hugs, Margaret watched

Lacy drive away. Margaret had lied to Lacy but felt she had no other recourse. Unable to look Lacy in the face and tell her the awful truth was something she just could not do.

The drive to Inner Harbour was uneventful, but she used the time for recording messages into her handheld recorder to review later. Pulling up in front of Aunt Mallory's house, she thought the house looked lonely and dark. Lacy pulled her bag from the car and slung her laptop bag over her shoulder. Pulling the key from her pocket, she opened the front door, turned on the light, and stopped. The room looked as it did in her dream with the furniture all covered.

"Don't be stupid Lacy, she told herself. Of course, it's going to be covered to protect it."

Dropping her bags by the door, she walked around the house remembering the few times she had been here. She loved the style of the house, and as she began pulling sheets off the furniture, she noticed that Aunt Mallory had amazing taste.

Placing all the sheets on a chair so she would remember to recover everything when she left, she decided her first priority was to sort out somewhere to sleep. Walking up the stairs, it hit her again that everything looked just like it did in her dream.

She walked to each door and opened it slowly, the furniture was all covered, and only the mattress lay on the bed. She had a weird feeling but told herself she was silly.

At the end of the hallway, the bedroom door was slightly ajar. As Lacy walked toward the room and opened the door further, she half expected to see her Aunt Mallory standing by the window. She wasn't, but this was the only room in the house where the furniture was uncovered, and the bed prepared. "That's strange, she thought, Gran must have called someone here in town to come over and get a room ready for me. That was sweet of her." She turned to go back down stairs to get her things, and she could swear she smelled Jovan perfume. The kind Aunt Mallory wore.

Back at Pleasant Cove, Margaret was sitting at her kitchen table with the notepad and pen. It seemed like she was writing for a very long time. It was vital that she put this all in here. Lacy had to know. The time flew by, and she didn't even realize she was crying until large wet tears dropped onto the page. Lifting her head, she felt drained, and her hand hurt from the grip on the pen.

She looked at the urn holding her dear friend and said, "Oh, Mallory what will she think when she knows the truth? Maybe I should have told her, but there was no way I could look into her in the face and say those words.

I can only hope she understands and can forgive me."

There was stillness in the room, and Margaret felt warmth touch her skin. She knew her friend was near.

As Lacy woke, she could hear the rain outside, and it sounded like drums beating. "Great, she thought. Now I've got to be traipsing around in the rain." She hoped Aunt Mallory left a raincoat in the closet because she didn't bring one. Lacy got out of bed and went to the bathroom to start her day. In the bathroom, Lacy found fresh towels in the closet and enjoyed a long hot shower. Feeling alive again she thought she would grab a coffee at the local coffee shop and see if there were any news buzzing around. After that, she would drop by and see Allan.

Rummaging through the closet, she found a raincoat, pulled it on, and ran to her car. She drove to the local coffee shop. If there were news, people would most likely be talking. However, people in small communities were usually friendly but closed at the same time. She was not from this community and that, at the very least, made her an outsider.

She pulled into a parking spot at the local coffee shop and was surprised to see how many people were inside. Didn't anyone have coffee at home anymore? She went in shaking the rain from her coat as she entered, found a small table somewhere in the middle of the room and sat down.

Before she could take her coat off, a server was

standing beside her with a menu and a coffee pot.

"Morning. What would you like?"

"Coffee and your breakfast special please." She wasn't hungry, but it would help her not stick out like a sore finger if she was sitting eating. Lifting the steaming hot cup of coffee was enjoyment enough, but the taste was fantastic. It had to be the best cup of coffee she ever had. She picked up a discarded newspaper and gave the illusion of reading it while she listened to the talk all around her.

One man was talking about his sheep, another about his tractor that just would not work, and another complaining about how much money his wife spent ordering stuff from the Sears book. If there was news about this Jarred Brown, she didn't think she would hear it in here. She leafed through the paper and continued listening when a voice from behind startled her.

"I don't believe that you're going to find any current news in that paper."

She spun around to see Allan standing behind her.

"That's an article from last week."

She looked at the date and chuckled, "dam I blew my cover."

He sat across from her and asked where she was

staying. She told him at her Aunt Mallory's house.

"Mallory Johnson's?"

"Yes. Why?"

"No reason, I didn't know Mallory had any family left."

"Well, she wasn't my real Aunt. She and my grandmother were best friends since childhood, and I just always called her that, actually, we all did. I came in here this morning, hoping I would hear some bit of news, but so far the steaming story is about how much one of the local women spends ordering from the Sears catalog."

"So, what do you know so far?" Lacy asked.

"Well, with what I told you on the phone and a bit of digging, not too much. Jarred Brown has been a part of this community his entire life. Linda Godfrey and her daughter moved here from Toronto after a nasty divorce. Of course, Jarred Brown is saying this is all a big misunderstanding. Folks here in the community are divided as you can imagine."

"Yes, I'm sure they would be."

"Well, I've got to get back to the office, drop by and see me later and let me know what you find out."

"Yes, I will, and thanks for the job Allan."

"Yup, no problem Lacy."

The server came and brought her breakfast and though she wasn't hungry when she ordered it, the smell was fantastic. Her rumbling stomach was glad she ordered the breakfast after all.

Halfway through her breakfast and getting tired of listening to the local chitchat, she heard the door open signaled by the tinkle of a bell. A man walked in, and the silence was deafening. He walked in, looked at everyone looking at him, and walked to a table in the back. Slowly whispers could be heard.

Lacy knew without having to ask who this was and what had just happened. Well, maybe a second cup of coffee was in order.

The server walked over and almost threw the menu at the man, and sloppily poured his coffee.

"I'll have my usual Mildred," he said.

Without responding, the server walked away with a look of disgust on her face.

The man unfolded the paper he carried under his arm and with shaking hands spread it out on the table. He seemed oblivious to the surrounding whispers around him.

It was not so much that he couldn't hear, but that he decided to ignore it.

She finished her breakfast, enjoyed the second cup of coffee, and waited to see what would happen. She didn't have to wait too long. Mildred brought the man's breakfast and came close to dumping it in his lap and walked away. Lacy noticed that not one person spoke to him and he shared his time or thoughts with no one. Lacy decided she knew where she was going to start and leaving the money and a generous tip on the table she left.

CHAPTER ELEVEN

Finding out where Linda Godfrey lived was not hard. The local phone book provided an address and a phone number, all of which Lacy marked in her book. She decided against calling first as she didn't want to give Linda the chance of turning her away on the phone. People were funny when it came to reporters or writers. Lacy understood this and never took it personally. Driving to the street that was listed in the phone book, she pulled up in front of a little house that had seen better days. As she got out of her car, she could smell the saltwater roses. It always amazed Lacy that these flowers grew so rapidly in the harsh weather of Newfoundland, but it seemed like they flourished not because of the constant salt water, but in spite of it. Her grandmother had them planted all over the family graveyard. It helped make the spot scenic as well as peaceful.

She walked up to the door and rang the bell.

A woman in her late thirties opened the door.

"Can I help you?"

"Mrs. Godfrey?"

"Yes."

"My name is Lacy Blanchard I was wondering if I could have a few minutes of your time to talk to you about Jarred Brown." The woman looked at her for several seconds and then opened the door for Lacy to enter.

"Can I ask your interest in this Ms. Blanchard?"

"Yes, of course. I've been asked by your local paper to prepare a story, and I thought the best place to start was with you if that's okay?"

"I've filed a report with our local police you could have spoken to them."

"I prefer the direct approach if at all possible."

"What would you like to know?"

"I understand that a local resident named Jarred Brown has had inappropriate contact with your daughter."

"Inappropriate contact, well, I guess that is one way of putting it, but the correct way is that bastard molested my daughter."

"How did you find out?"

"Sam told me. She has been having nightmares for a couple of years, but I mostly thought it was because she missed her Dad, and the divorce was hard on her. I never dreamed it was something like this."

"I can only imagine."

"No. Not unless you have had a daughter yourself. There is no way you can understand the feeling of being a bad mother. And asking yourself how could I not know, and knowing no matter how bad you feel can't compare to what she must be feeling."

"I'm sorry. You're right. Where is Sam's father?"

"He died five years ago in a car accident. He had a hard time accepting the divorce. He was out drinking and took a bend too fast, he hit a transport truck head on, and he died instantly."

"I'm so sorry."

"Thanks."

"Mrs. Godfrey, I want to protect your daughter as much as I can in the reporting of this story and because she is still a minor her name won't be used. You must know that news spreads like wildfire in small communities."

"One of the reasons I came to this town was because I thought it would be a safe place to raise my daughter."

"And the other reasons?"

"Are my own."

The two woman looked at each other, one deciding if she could trust this person, the other trying to decide how she was going to get to the bottom of this without hurting this person, who apparently wanted to keep her private life just that.

"May I ask how long your daughter said the abuse was going on?"

"Sam said the first time was when she was ten. She was selling Girl Guide cookies, and he asked her to come into his house and began talking to her. Jarred bought six boxes and said she was the prettiest Girl Guide he had ever seen, and if she couldn't sell all the cookies to come back and see him and he would buy what she had left. She was delighted, of course, because she wanted to sell the most cookies. When she was leaving, he gave her a hug, and he slipped his hand under her little skirt. She didn't know how to react to this and never told me."

"I thought his offer to buy the rest of her cookies was rather sweet and went over to thank him for being so kind to my little girl. He said it was his pleasure. He seemed like a nice man. Over time, he became a close neighbor and friend.

He had no children of his own, and he appeared to take a keen interest in Sam. Jarred would talk to her like she was so important, ask about her day at school and her friends. I was glad she had a male friend to look up to. Little did I know he was just paving the way."

"When I started working as a waitress, my shift wouldn't end until 6 p.m. Jarred was here visiting when I got the call for the job. I had to turn it down because I didn't have anyone to watch Sam from the time she got out of school until I got home. Jarred was quick to tell me to get on the phone and call them back and say I could take the job. He said there was no reason why he couldn't keep an eye on Sam for a few hours. He had nothing better to do, and he said he enjoyed her company. So, you see, Ms. Blanchard, I gave him my child on a platter."

"No. Mrs. Godfrey, you trusted someone who pretended to be helpful and considered a friend. I can't say I ever experienced anything close to what your daughter has endured, but a situation with my music teacher many years ago gives me a small idea."

The two women looked at each other, and it seemed like an unspoken understanding had formed.

"Stop with the Mrs., it makes me feel old. My name is Linda, and if I'm going to divulge so much personal information to you, I'm just going to call you Lacy. Fair enough?"

"Fair enough."

"Would you like a cup of tea Lacy?"

"I would, thank you."

The two women sat and talked over a hot pot of tea, and it seemed the conversation continued of its own accord to other things. Before she knew it, almost two hours had passed.

"My goodness, I didn't mean to take up this much of your time. I'm so sorry."

"That's okay. I enjoyed talking with you. What will you do with the information I gave you?"

"Well, I will try to speak to Jarred Brown and see what his side is. My job, is to report the facts without taking sides, and to be objective."

"I understand."

The two women said their goodbyes, each left with unanswered questions to ponder. Lacy felt sorry for Linda and her daughter. Sorry for what Samantha went through, and sorry for Linda for feeling like she failed her daughter. She was surprised at how long they sat and talked. Linda seemed like a nice woman even if she were a little mysterious.

As she drove her car into the driveway, Lacy had a strange feeling of being watched.

She told herself she was just being silly, gathered up her things, and went inside the house where it felt wonderfully warm after the cold rain. She discarded her things on the sofa and went upstairs to put on some dry, comfortable clothes with the plans of getting started on her story.

As she walked up the stairs, she caught the soft smell of Jovan. She guessed that Aunt Mallory's perfume was ingrained in the house. It was a comfortable feeling. She changed and went back downstairs just as her cell phone started ringing.

"Hello."

"Hi yourself, I was just getting ready to leave you a message."

"Hi, John, I'm sorry I didn't get to call you before I left It was kind of last-minute assignment."

"That's okay. I was calling to tell you I have to go out of town myself for a few days on business in New York. I'll be back by the weekend. If your schedule should allow it, maybe we could have dinner?"

"That would be nice. Call me when you get back."

"Okay. Talk to you later."

They said their goodbyes and Lacy wondered if there was ever going to be a future with John Sinclair. Not that she was ready to settle down just yet.

But a girl could wonder. Couldn't she?

She went to the kitchen and made herself a cup of tea, brought it back to the living room and found herself smiling at the beautiful memory of the tea parties she used to have with her grandmother when she was a little girl. She always felt so special, Her grandmother would make a pot of tea in her best china teapot, and they would drink tea in the beautiful china cups. Once she asked her grandmother if she were afraid to use such beautiful cups in case she would break one. Her gran had told her that a tea party with her granddaughter was more important than a broken teacup. Lacy always tried to be extra careful when she held it.

Sitting cross-legged on the sofa Lacy opened up her notebook and flipped the cover open on her laptop, she had to start on the first part of this story.

As she was making notes and working on her story, Lacy began to wonder what this Jarred Brown was like. Who was he? She looked at what she had written so far and knew she couldn't go any further without speaking to Jarred. Looking up at the clock it showed 4:15 p.m. She decided it was time to meet Mr. Jarred Brown, she went upstairs and changed her clothes.

His house was not hard to find, she looked up the information when she found Linda's. He was just one street over.

She pulled up in front of the house, slipped her small

recorder in her pocket and walked up to the front door, knocked, and heard some shuffling as someone walked toward the door. An old man hunched a little, with the coldest gray eyes Lacy had ever seen, opened the door just a few inches.

"Mr. Brown?"

"Who wants to know?"

"My name is Lacy Blanchard. I'm a freelance writer and I'm doing a job for your local newspaper and was wondering if perhaps I could speak to you for a few minutes."

His eyes bore into her, and it made her cold to the bottom of her heart. She did not like the feeling she was getting from this man.

"Mr. Brown, you have some charges brought against you, and I would like to get your side of the story if I could."

He glared at her for a few minutes, but he opened the door.

"What side is it you are you interested in Miss Blanchard? My side is Samantha is lying. I don't know why and I don't care why, but she is lying."

"I see."

"I tried to be a good neighbor to Linda and Sam, help

out when she got that job as a waitress, and this is the thanks I get."

"Mr. Brown, why do you think Samantha Godfrey would lie about such a thing?"

"I don't know, and I don't care. My lawyer will prove that I'm innocent."

He kept staring at her so intently it was making her feel uncomfortable.

"You look very familiar to me, but you're not from around here."

"No, I'm not. I live in Clancy, but my grandmother was born here in Inner Harbour."

"Your grandmother?"

"Yes, Her name is Margaret Blanchard, and her maiden name was Wilson."

She saw the look change in his eyes.

"Well, well, Margaret Wilson's granddaughter!"

"You know my grandmother?"

"Yes, I knew her when she lived here in Inner Harbour."

"Really. I asked my grandmother if she knew you.

She said she couldn't recall anyone by the name of Jarred Brown."

He chuckled, and it was not a pleasant sound.

"Oh, we knew each other for sure."

"Well, it has been many years, I'm sure she just forgot."

"Perhaps."

"Well, Mr. Brown, thank you for your time, I've got to be going."

"Be sure and tell your grandmother I said hi."

"Yes, I will. Goodbye Mr. Brown and thank you for speaking with me."

Lacy felt like she just walked through spider webs and she could not get out of there fast enough. It was an awful feeling, and she knew without anyone having to tell her that this man was guilty.

Margaret was tired today. She had stayed up late last night writing in her notebook, feeling like she had to get everything wrote down. Hoping with all her heart that Lacy would understand and one day forgive her for lying to her. The pain in her chest radiated down her arm and didn't want to leave, these past few days. She decided she would make an appointment with her doctor. Maybe she pulled a muscle when she was gardening.

She had not heard from Lacy since she went to Inner Harbour, and she was too much of a chicken to call and see how things were going. She hoped she was okay.

"Oh, Mallory, I would hate for her to know the truth or for Michael to find out such vileness about his mother. They deserve to know the truth, and I'm just so sorry I can't have the guts to tell them face to face."

As if someone whispered in her ear, she heard someone say,

"You'll do the right thing."

Silly, she knew, but she felt like Mallory was talking to her. This day seemed like it had no end and the pain was getting worse.

"I think I'll make an early night of it after I write a bit more. I'm almost done anyway," she thought.

She sat herself at the table and began to write, words flowing across the page. Finally, exhausted and in much pain, she laid the pen aside. It was done. The truth had been written. She would give this final gift to her granddaughter.

Back at the house, while working on her story, Lacy had the strange feeling that she needed to get back home. She couldn't shake the feeling that something was wrong with her grandmother.

There was no answer when she called several times this evening and ended up leaving a message. It was funny that her gran didn't call her back. She emailed the story to Allan and then called him.

"Hi Allan, I've just emailed the article to you."

"Thanks, Lacy, I really appreciate it. So I guess you got to talk to Mr. Brown?"

"Yes, I did, and I can say that I don't think I like him very much. He seems very, cold."

"It's true, that he is not well liked by many people."

"Well, I'm going to be heading back in the morning, so just pop the check in the mail will you Allan?"

"I Will Lacy, and thanks again."

They said their goodbyes and hung up.

She walked through the house gathering things. She tried to call her grandmother again, and again there was no answer.

"Maybe she's out visiting, she thought. I'll see her in the morning. I'm going to get some sleep and start out early."

She packed her things and laid them by the door, all she had to do in the morning was to dress, and go.

She got into bed and lay on her side, staring out at the

big white moon in the sky she drifted off to sleep. Her sleep was troubled this night, filled with dreams and visions.

The smell of Jovan woke her. She sat up in bed and looked around. There was a light in the hallway, but she was sure she had turned it off. She got out of bed and walked into the hall. Standing by the window was her Aunt Mallory. The moonlight glowing through the window made her vapor like.

"She needs you, Lacy, you have to go to her now. She loves you so very much."

Lacy turned and look back into the room, when she turned around again, there was nothing there. She had been dreaming of course, but she couldn't shake the strange feeling. It was strong, and it was overwhelming. Lacy needed to get to her grandmother. She thought perhaps she should call her father, but she was most likely over reacting to a dream, so why wake him up. It was almost 5 a.m., and her since grandmother was an early riser, she would probably be sitting having her breakfast when Lacy got there.

She would tell her gran about the dream, and they would laugh about how silly she had been. Dressing quickly, she left a note for the friend of her grandmothers' saying she was sorry but couldn't clean up, as she had to leave in a hurry. Within twenty minutes, she was on the road to her grandmothers, and if she had looked in her rear view mirror, she might have seen a woman looking out the window watching her go.

If she had turned around and went back inside she may have seen all the furniture covered in white sheets, the fridge door standing open emptied of all its contents the doors to all the bedrooms standing open and all the beds bare of sheets and covers. If she had gone back, she would have wondered if she had been there at all.

CHAPTER TWELVE

Lacy knew the roads well, and so she made excellent time. She pulled into her grandmother's driveway at 6:20 a.m., got out of the car, walked to the door, and turned the knob knowing it was not going to be locked. The house was silent, and she felt uneasy.

"Gran are you up?"

There was no answer just the stillness of the house. She walked down the hall toward the bathroom and listened for the sound of the shower. It was soundless. She slowly walked toward her grandmothers' bedroom and saw her on the floor with her hand on her chest.

"OH my God Gran!"

She rushed to her, but something inside of her knew she was too late. Laying her hand on her grandmother's face, she felt cold.

Picking up the phone from the nightstand, she called

her grandmothers' doctor who said he would come immediately. Then, she called her parents who stated that they were leaving immediately. Back in her grandmothers' room, Lacy sat on the floor and gently lifted her in her arms. With sobs wrenching her body she pleaded, "Please Gran, don't leave me."

When the doctor arrived, he found Lacy sitting on the floor holding her grandmother. It was a scene that would touch his heart for the rest of his life. Gently he spoke to Lacy, and together they laid Margaret on the bed. He asked Lacy to put on some tea and give him a few minutes to examine her grandmother. She reluctantly left the room her body wrenching with sobs from her broken heart. She knew now why she had such a feeling of needing to come to her grandmother. Why didn't she come sooner?

She didn't feel like tea, but it would keep her hands busy. She heard her parents' car as they drove up. Funny how the time flies, it seemed like only seconds ago she had called. Her parents came in, and she flew into her mothers' arms and cried, as she never cried before. What was she going to do without her grandmother? She remembered when her grandfather died, it hurt, but she had never felt lost like she was feeling now. She wanted to die from the heartbreak. Her mother tried to console her, her father wrapped his arms around her, and her heart broke again when she heard her father sobbing.

"We'll get through this Lacy. She made us strong, and now we have to be strong."

Doctor Edging knew Margaret Blanchard for almost twenty-five years, and he liked and respected her.

"I'm so sorry for your loss. It appears Margaret had a heart attack, and though it's of small consequence I can assure you, your mother did not suffer. It was very quick. I'll take care of things here Michael."

"Thank you, doctor."

The next few hours went by quickly. The ambulance came and took Margaret away, neighbors came and went, and all the time Lacy felt like this was all a terrible dream. She was going to wake up, and she was going to find her grandmother in the kitchen, but she didn't wake up because it was not a dream. Her grandmother was gone. How would she get along without her?

It was late in the day when her parents said they needed to get back to the city. There were things that needed to be taken care of and arrangements made.

"I'm going to stay, said Lacy. I need to be here right now."

Her parents looked at each other, and her Mother walked over to her and put her arms around her.

"Lacy, you know your grandmother would not want you to blame yourself for not being here. There was no way to know. She was old, and she lived a long and beautiful life."

"I know Mom; I just feel like I need to be here."

"I'll call you in the morning with the details for the service okay."

"Thanks, Dad."

They hugged and kissed and as her parents left. Once again, she heard the quietness of the house.

There was peace in this house. This was her real home, and she decided no matter what, she was never going to let go of this place, never let go of her grandmother. She walked through the house touching things that have been a part of her entire life, but before this moment had never given much thought to them. She brushed her hands over the picture of her grandparents on their wedding day, another of her grandmother and Aunt Mallory in school uniforms, and another of her grandmother holding her when she was born. She was looking up so intently into the eyes of the woman who would form her spirit and soul. Lacy knew a bond had developed between her and her grandmother. It was a bond never broken.

Her head hurt from all the crying, she took a couple of aspirin and decided to go to her grandmothers' bedroom. Lying on the bed, she stared out the window.

"Oh, Gran, did you know how much I loved you? Did you know that you made my world complete? How do I go on without you?"

Exhaustion finally overcame her, and she drifted off to sleep. She was surrounded by darkness, and then slowly the stars seemed to be all around her, their brilliance lighting a path. Walking on the starlit path, in the distance, she saw a man and a woman embracing. She could hear their conversation, but their lips were not moving.

"I told you I would wait," she heard the man say. Then the woman turned around. It was her grandmother.

"Gran?"

"Yes, Lacy it's me. I'm sorry I had to leave you so soon my darling, but I'll always be with you. Know that I'm happy and that I love you with all of my heart."

"But Gran I don't understand."

"Remember what I told you, Lacy, nothing lasts forever, nothing good and nothing bad and that goes for people as well."

Just then, another woman walked up and joined them. It was her Aunt Mallory.

"We'll take care of her for you Lacy."

"Lacy I hope you can forgive me for what I've done. I know I should have told you before, but I just couldn't."

"Forgive you? For what?"

"I wrote it all down for you Lacy, in the notebook you gave me. Find it, and please forgive me."

She kissed her on the face and was gone. Lacy woke with a start and knew her grandmother had come to say goodbye to her. She knew she had visited her in her dream. But what was she talking about? What notebook? And why would her grandmother be asking for her forgiveness?

She got out of bed, wrapped herself in a blanket, and went to the kitchen. The time on the clock said 3:00 a.m. Her head still hurt, and she felt drained. Walking to the rocking chair, she sat down. The moonlight over the water was beautiful. No wonder her grandmother loved this place. It was a small part of heaven on earth.

She noticed her grandmother had moved her Aunt Mallory's ashes on the shelf close to the chair. She smiled, knowing how like her grandmother that was. Lacy turned her head toward the table where she did her homework as a child and had so many wonderful dinners with her grandmother and her eyes fell on the notebook.

She slowly got up, walked to the table, picked up the book, and opened the cover and began to read.

"My Darling Lacy, if you are reading this then I have gone to join your grandfather and Aunt Mallory. I want to ask your forgiveness for lying to you the day you came to me and asked me about Jarred Brown. I should have told you the truth then, but I was too ashamed. Now I need to the right the wrong. The fact is I did know a Jarred Brown when I was a girl. Though, I can tell you with all my heart that I wish I did not. It started back when …"

Lacy read for hours and cried for the shame this awful man had caused her beautiful grandmother. She felt so sorry for the little girl who was so hurt. She understood why her grandmother did not say she knew Jarred Brown. The shame would have been too much for her to bear.

"Lacy I know your book will be a success. Not because it is about my life but because you are an amazing, gifted writer. So in closing here is the final gift I can offer to your book. Use it if you will or not. It is your choice."

"To my darling granddaughter Lacy... I'll walk just beyond the moon, then I'll stop and wait for you."

"As in all things, nothing lasts forever, nothing good and nothing bad. A story of a life lived is history."

"I hope the history of my life reads of a woman who loved her family and all things beautiful. One day I hope my history story begins with Long ago, there lived a woman who loved God with all her heart and the journey of her life is amazing..."

I will always watch over you,

Love your Gran.

CHAPTER THIRTEEN

Lacy closed the cover of the notebook and sat looking out toward the water, as her gran did for so many years. The sound of the phone ringing startled her, it was John. Her parents had called him, and he said how sorry he was for her loss, and he would cut his business trip short to be home with her for the funeral.

"No John, please don't do that. There isn't going to be a big ceremony, just a few close friends of the family and I'll be fine."

"Okay, Lacy, but if you need me just call me. I know how much she meant to you."

"Thank you, John."

They spoke for a short while longer, and the conversation ended as usual, with equal politeness. Lacy's parents were the next to call asking how she was doing and to let her know that the funeral would take place the day after tomorrow.

She said she was doing okay, that she was finding comfort from just being here. She ended the call with I love you, and I'll see you tomorrow. She made a cup of tea and tried to prepare herself for all the people who would be coming to pay their respect, and with their condolences, came casseroles, cakes, cookies, sandwiches, and soups. Her parents arrived about two hours later, and that took some pressure off her. She just needed some quiet, and she slipped into her grandmother's bedroom without notice. Lying on the bed that she had found comfort in as a child, it now gave support to the grown, grieving granddaughter of the woman who was such a huge part of her world.

Was this pain what her gran had felt when she lost her grandfather and Aunt Mallory? If so, she didn't know how she got the courage to go on. Exhaustion finally gave in, and she fell asleep for a few hours. When she woke, it was dark outside, and the house was quiet. She rose and went out into the kitchen where her parents were sitting drinking tea.

"Sit baby, I'll get you a cup of tea."

"Thanks, Mom."

"I'm sorry I fell asleep and left you alone with all those people."

"Your mom and I are going to stay here tonight there is no point in driving all the way back to town for a few hours."

"I'm glad you're here," said Lacy.

They talked and shared stories, laughed, and cried. The toll of the day had taken its hold on everyone. They retired for the night. Morning would come fast enough.

The morning came, with the sun a beautiful shade of pink as the dawn was preparing for its day. Lacy lay, looking out the window, she felt like this was still a bad dream, but she knew it was real. She had lost the one person whom she loved most in the world besides her parents. Now, she didn't know how this would affect her world. Her grandmother always said, When you're left with no choice you deal with what's left. She was the granddaughter of Margaret Blanchard, and as such, she would conduct herself accordingly.

Her parents were still asleep, so she quietly got up, showered, and slipped into the black dress her mother had brought her. She was making coffee when her parents entered the kitchen. Her father was wearing his black suit and her mom her gray and black dress. If one didn't know the circumstances, you would think they were all going to a formal affair. They sat for a while and drank their coffee and then her mother said, "It's time for us to go."

They walked out of the house to go the church for the service. Lacy felt like she was going to pass out and stumbled a little and her father caught her by the arm.

"I know it's going to be a rough day for all of us baby girl," said her dad.

The church was filled with people, everyone wanting to say a kind word or two. Then the service started. She went through the motions but didn't really hear much of the service. She was lost in the past where her grandmother was alive, and she was telling one of her beautiful stories. Then she realized there would be no more stories, no more tea parties, no more Gran. The service had ended with the priest saying that only family members would attend at the graveside and everyone else was invited to join the family at the local hall for the reception.

They waited until the church emptied before getting ready to remove the casket. Lacy and her parents walked up to the casket and looked down at the woman who had touched more lives than she probably ever knew. Lacy opened her bag and gently placed aunt Mallory's earn near her grandmothers' arms.

"We promised you Gran, and so you and Aunt Mallory will be together forever."

"Father, would you please wait until we leave before you close the lid?"

"Of course, Mr. Blanchard, I understand."

They turned and walked out of the church, got into their car and drove to the graveside.

The sunlight fell upon the coffin as it was removed from the hearse.

The casket was magnificent white that it was almost blinding to look at.

"Mom, you and Dad did an excellent job."

"Thank you, dear, as far as coffins go I think your gran would have like the color."

They both gave a small chuckle because that is exactly what Gran would have said.

The service was short, the flowers laid, it was time to go to the reception. Lacy really didn't want to go, but it was all part of this sad day. She and her parents walked in, and everyone was so kind. Out of the corner of her eye, Lacy saw Mandy coming toward her. With huge hugs, both women cried.

"I'm so sorry Lacy. I know what she meant to you."

"Thank you, Mandy, and thank you for coming."

"Of course," said Mandy.

They talked for a few minutes more and then Lacy had to excuse herself to speak to some other people. They made plans to get together soon. The reception seemed like it was going to go on for hours, but eventually, everyone left, and they went back to the house, all three exhausted and sad.

Sitting in the living room, each with their own memories of the amazing woman they had just lost, Lacy couldn't wait any longer.

"Dad, I know this is hardly the time to bring this up, but if I don't say something now, I'm afraid it may be to late."

"Say what Darling?"

"Well I know as Grans' only son you automatically get her estate, but Dad, you can't sell this house, you just can't."

Her parents looked at one another, and her mom said,

"Go on tell her."

"Tell me what?"

"Well, as it turns out, Lacy I couldn't sell this house even if I wanted to."

"Why?"

"Because, silly girl, your gran left it to you. It's your house now Lacy."

"Oh, my God! I can't believe it," and then the tears started again.

"There are some other things we need to discuss, but it can wait I think we should turn in now. I for one am exhausted," said Lacy's dad.

Snuggled under the blankets in her grandmothers' bed, Lacy felt sad, but so safe. This beautiful house was hers now, though she would always think of it as her grandmothers.

"Thank you, Gran," she softly whispered.

As much as she just wanted to watch the moon in the night sky, her body, mind, and soul were exhausted, and she was soundly asleep within minutes of her mumbled thanks to her grandmother. This night she slept soundly, there were no dreams, no nightmares, and no visits from her gran.

Dawn broke getting ready for a new day. Lacy knew it was going to be yet another hard one. A song she once heard called **When I'm Gone,** by Joey and Rory Feek, was playing in her head, and she softly, and quietly sang the song, with tears running down her cheeks onto her grandmothers' pillow.

*Ownership of this song belongs to

{Joey and Rory Feek}

When I'm Gone

A bright sunrise will contradict the heavy fault that weighs you down. In spite of all the funeral songs, the birds will make their joyful sounds. You wonder why the earth still moves. You wonder how you'll carry on, but you'll be okay on that first day when I'm gone.

Dusk will come with fireflies and whippoorwill, and crickets call. And every star will take its place, with silvery gown and purple shawl. You'll lie down in our big bed dread the dark and dread the dawn, but you'll be all right on that first night when I'm gone.

You will reach for me in vain, you'll be whispering my name, as if sorrow were your friend, and this world so in the end. But life will call with daffodils, and morning glorious blue skies. You'll think of me some memory, and softly smile to your surprise.

And even though you love me still, you will know where you belong. Just give it time we'll both be fine when I'm gone.

The words of that song fit so well with her life right now, and they were words her grandmother would say for sure. She dried her face, pushed the warm covers off, got up, and quietly got her shower before her parents rose. They would be going back to the city today. She went to the kitchen and made coffee, not bothering to put on a light, she walked over to her grans' rocking chair; coffee cup clasped in both hands, rocked, and looked out into the dawning day.

This would be a day without her grandmother. It was a very sobering thought. Her parents walked into the kitchen and turned the light on.

"Oh, you're up, and made coffee already."

"Yeah, just needed some quiet time I guess."

Her parents came in and sat on the sofa. They were worried about her.

"Lacy, why don't you come home with us for awhile, just until we've all had time to get through this."

"Thanks Dad, but going home with you and Mom is not going to change the fact that Gran is gone. Many times Gran told me when you're left with no choice, you deal with what left, and I guess I have to do that in my own way."

"Lacy, I don't think it's a good idea for you to stay here right now. It's all too fresh, all too much to deal with alone."

"I'm never alone Mom. Gran will always be with me, and right now, I need to be here. You and Dad go on home, I'll call you later tonight, I promise."

They finished their coffee, and with hugs and kisses, she sent her parents on their way. Home, where was that for her now?

She always felt at home here, because her grandmother was always here. Now she was alone. She knew some things needed doing, but she couldn't face all of it at once. She walked into her grandmothers' bedroom and sat on the bed.

"Oh, Gran, what am I supposed to do now?"

Lacy stayed at the cottage in the cove for the rest of the week. She packed up her grandmothers' clothes, some books, and odds and ends to go to the goodwill store. She placed her grandmothers' jewelry box and anything of value in a box to take with her.

She had arranged for Bridget Collier to keep the house cleaned every couple of weeks. Her father called throughout the week and yes, the house, and everything in it was hers now. But to her, it would always be her grandmothers' house. Her father told her about the trust fund that was set up for her. It took her by surprise.

Her grandmother had told her dad that she wanted the money there for Lacy so she wouldn't have to take so many freelance jobs and could focus on her writing. Just like her gran, selfless to the end. There was just one thing left to do. She took her grandmother's sweater off the chair and went out the back door, up the path that she only had visited a few days before.

Sitting on the same bench her gran had sat on for so many years, she closed her eyes and tried to calm her soul.

Everything in her was rushing and going in slow motion all at the same time. She opened her eyes and looked up to the sky.

It was a brilliant blue, and the sun seemed brighter today as well.

Swallowing the lump in her throat, she started to talk to her grandmother.

"Hi, Gran. I know you are at rest and happy to be with Grandpa and Aunt Mallory, but I miss you so much. It's like a part of me is missing, and I'm not sure how I'm going to make it without you. You raised me to be strong, and I don't know where that strength will come from, but I'll find it. I'm going back to my apartment today. I know you left the house to me. Thank you for that and everything you've ever done for me. I love you so much Gran, and I'll be back, I'm just not sure when. Maybe when the pain fades a little."

She kissed the beautiful headstone that bore her grandmothers' name. *Margaret Blanchard, Beloved Wife, Mother, and Grandmother.*

"You were all this and so much more Gran.

She took a final walk through the house that was such a huge part of her life printing to memory all the good times she shared here with her grandmother, and now it was time. Her bag was packed and placed by the door. She opened the door and took one final look around, her eyes fell to her grandmothers' rocking chair, and she softly whispered, "Goodbye Gran I'll see you soon, I love you."

She put her bags in the car, tears streaming down her face and began her drive back to her apartment in Clancy.

It was hard for her to believe your heart can hurt so much, yet you are able to breathe. She thought about all the tapes that she made with her grandmother and realized what an amazing gift she had.

She turned on the radio for company and just pressed the seek button, she didn't care what she listened to, she just needed the distraction.

The radio stopped on an old country station called The Grand Old Opry. The radio announcer had a Texan voice.

"Folks, when I awoke this morning, there was a song playing in my head. I don't know why, but it's stuck with me all day, so I guess I'm supposed to share it with you. Maybe somebody somewhere is meant to hear this song. It's a beautiful Tex Ritter Song, called *Just beyond the Moon.*"

(RECITATION)

MY MOTHER AND MY FATHER WERE IN LOVE FOR 50 YEARS. SO, WHEN DAD DIED, WE WONDERED WHY OUR MOTHER SHED NO TEARS. WE ASKED HER ONCE ABOUT IT, BUT SHE WOULDN'T TELL US WHY, INSTEAD, SHE'D WALK OUTSIDE EACH NIGHT AND SMILE UP AT THE SKY.

THEN JUST BEFORE SHE LEFT US SHE CALLED US TO HER SIDE AND SHE TOLD US WHAT OUR FATHER SAID TO HER JUST BEFORE HE DIED.

(Song:)

I REMEMBER WHEN YOU SAID YOU'D NEVER LEAVE ME. THROUGH THESE GOLDEN YEARS, I'VE KEPT THE SAME VOW TOO. BUT NOW THAT I AM GOING PLEASE DON'T LEAVE ME. I'LL WALK JUST BEYOND THE MOON THEN I'LL STOP AND WAIT FOR YOU.

YOU CAN LOOK UP EVERY NIGHT, AND YOU'LL SEE ME LIGHT THE LIGHT, WHERE I'LL WATCH FOR YOU TO JOIN ME SOMEDAY SOON. WE'LL GO LOOKIN THROUGH THE STARS FOR THE HEAVEN THAT IS OURS, AND I KNOW WE'LL FIND IT SOON SOMEWHERE JUST BEYOND THE MOON.

I'LL JUST SIT THERE BY A STAR AND I'LL WATCH YOU FROM AFAR TIL I SEE YOU WALKING TOWARD ME SOMEDAY SOON. THEN TOGETHER HAND IN HAND, WE'LL FIND OUR PROMISED LAND, AND WE'LL SETTLE DOWN FOREVER DARLIN' JUST BEYOND THE MOON.

Lacy pulled the car over to the side of the road and turned up the radio. The song began and with each note tears fell down her cheeks. It was a beautiful song. It was a song of love that withstood the passing of death and into the hereafter.   For Lacy, it was her grandmother telling her goodbye for now.

The song ended, she pulled some tissue out of her bag wiped her eyes, and blew her nose.

"Thank you for that gift Gran. I'll watch for that moon and for you until we meet again."

With the car back on the road to home, she found herself singing Just Beyond The Moon.

The Story of Margaret

ABOUT THE AUTHOR

Darlene Barry was born in St. Georges, NL, Lived in Ontario for 23 years and returned to the Island in 2011 where she finished The Story of Margaret. Darlene has many more books in the works, including Moonbeam, the follow up to Margaret. Be sure to look for them wherever books and eBooks are sold.